The Nine Lives of Jacob Tibbs

The NINE LIVES of JACOB TIBBS

CYLIN BUSBY

Illustrated by Gerald Kelley

A Yearling Book

 Published in the United States by Yearling, an imprint of Random House Children's Books, a division of Penguin Random House LLC, New York. Originally published in hardcover in the United States by Alfred A. Knopf, an imprint of Random House Children's Books, New York, in 2016.

Yearling and the jumping horse design are registered trademarks of Penguin Random House LLC.

Visit us on the Web! randomhousekids.com

Educators and librarians, for a variety of teaching tools, visit us at RHTeachersLibrarians.com

The Library of Congress has cataloged the hardcover edition of this work as follows:
Busby, Cylin, author.
The nine lives of Jacob Tibbs / Cylin Busby ; illustrated by Gerald Kelley. — First edition.
pages cm.
Summary: "The story of cat Jacob Tibbs, runt of the litter, and his exploits on the high seas as a ship's mouser." —Provided by publisher
ISBN 978-0-553-51123-9 (trade) — ISBN 978-0-553-51124-6 (lib. bdg.) —
ISBN 978-0-553-51125-3 (ebook)
[1. Cats—Fiction. 2. Seafaring life—Fiction. 3. Adventure and adventurers—Fiction.]
I. Kelley, Gerald, illustrator. II. Title.
PZ10.3.B955Ni 2016
[Fic]—dc23
2015012040

ISBN 978-0-553-51126-0 (pbk.)

Printed in the United States of America
10 9 8 7 6 5 4 3 2 1
First Yearling Edition 2017

For Melanie

CHAPTER 1

A LIFE BELOW

I was born on a ship, the runt of a six-litter. I didn't mind hearing myself called a runt, as that's what I was. And besides which, being smallest turned out to be my good fortune. My mother was a ship's cat to Captain Nicholas Natick, and she had spent a good many of her days on board the *Melissa Rae*—his ship named after his own daughter. The *Melissa Rae* was in port in Liverpool on the stormy gray day when my three sisters, two brothers, and I were born in the year 1847.

This was not my mother's first litter, and some of the sailors say she knew how to time herself to the docking of the ship, so as to not give birth on a stormy sea or interrupt her work as a captain's cat, which she took very seriously. Captain Natick dubbed my mother Mrs. Tibbs; he was a man who believed that those given a Christian name had a soul, and he wasn't one to partake of nicknames. So although the sailors sometimes called my mother Mrs. T., and later called me just Tibbs for short, you'd never hear the captain call us by anything other than our proper names.

For this reason, as soon as my siblings and I could open our eyes, the captain set about naming us as well, with the help of his daughter, Melissa. I'm sorry to say I was too young at the time, and many years have since passed, for me to remember everyone's name, but I do recall that I had one sister called Samantha, another named Butterscotch, and a brother of the name Moxie. I was called Jacob, which was Melissa's idea. She said if she'd been lucky enough to have had a brother, she would have wanted him to be called Jacob, and so it was.

The *Melissa Rae* was a sound ship, with a square stern and three masts. She was not a pretty craft, like the turned-out clippers with sails full up, but a working vessel, making the journey between England and America to deliver mail, packages, and whatever else she was hired out to carry. She traveled well, and the sailors on board gave due credit to my mother for their good fortune. My mother was no ordinary cat-o'-sea; she had a reputation that preceded her. And thus Mrs. Tibbs's kittens were regarded as lucky cats to have on board any seagoing vessel. So, after our naming, news traveled fast around Liverpool, and all the way to Manchester, that Mrs. T. had delivered a healthy litter of superb kittens. And since many other boats were in dock, waiting out the same weather as the *Melissa Rae*, we had quite a few visitors. Our fame was such that my siblings and I would probably all be claimed many days before we could even leave our own mother.

Of course, we were unaware of the bidding that went on above our heads, and those first days below deck were splendid. I thought our basket in the galley—what we sailors call the kitchen on the ship—was the whole world. The captain saw to it that my mother had plenty of fresh fish, and as a result, my siblings and I had plenty of milk. We napped in the sway of the great ship and played in the gray light below quarters. The sailors who came to look on us brought lanterns, for they could not see in the dark as we could.

During the day, the captain's daughter, Melissa, would sit with us for hours, petting us each in turn and bringing new bits of cotton and wool for Mrs. Tibbs's basket. When we were barely a week old, Melissa brought a piece of cloth, a calico, for us. Being so well washed and worn, it was nearly as soft as my mother. "Here you are, Mrs. Tibbs," Melissa said, tucking it around us. "I've brought you my favorite dress. I'm too big for it now, so I thought your little ones might have use of it." This cloth not only smelled of Melissa—a clean scent of some flowery soap—but made for a warm and cozy bed, especially when Mother had to leave us unattended for any length of time.

Melissa and Mrs. Tibbs got on quite grand, and they would spend a good spell of time in each other's company when we were in port. Melissa was a frail child and had a rattling cough that was aggravated by too much physical activity. Sitting in the galley of the ship with Mrs. Tibbs and us kittens brought her joy without putting a strain on her health. Captain Natick worried for her a great deal, and could be heard to say that for a girl without a mother, Melissa certainly had a soft hand with God's creatures. He would look on and sigh, and his ice-blue eyes would get a bit watery watching his daughter with us.

Our other visitors in port were the sailors from nearby ships, and some captains, as well, who came to purchase us from Captain Natick. These men were big and loud, and smelled of the sea. Like Captain Natick, most of them wore a captain's hat, and those who had hair wore it in a small braid at the back. They were not gentle with us and inspected us quite roughly. They would come, each in his turn, and talk a bit to Captain Natick before they were led below the deck—with lanterns lighting the way through the narrow passage—to our basket, which was tucked behind the stove in the galley. "Ah, Mrs. Tibbs, you've outdone yourself, haven't you?" they could be heard to say. My mother would purr and lift her head to be scratched behind the ears. Even at this early age, it made me proud to see so many great men show my mother such respect.

Butterscotch was the first to be spoken for. She was the biggest, and resembled my mother a good deal with the same white stripes, but instead of my mother's warm yellow fur, Butterscotch's was a rich orange. I remember her to have a mark on her forehead, yellow fur in an *M* shape over her eyes. A handsome mark for any cat, and as one sailor who saw her said, "She's got the *M* of Mrs. T. on 'er head; she's a lucky one there!" I hope her life was happy and long, though I never did hear of her again.

Samantha was the next to go, spoken for by a sailor on errand for his captain. "We'll take the gray, the frisky one." And Sam was indeed frisky! Always first to nurse and last to nap, she was bound for a life pacing the deck of a fine ship, I have little doubt.

A bearded captain called Mr. Russ took one brother and one sister with him; their names escape me. At the steep prices Captain Natick could ask, this was quite an investment. But Captain Russ had two ships, and he needed a new cat for each. "None better than those born of Mrs. T.," he said, then added with a cough, "Mrs. Tibbs, I mean to say. No disrespect, ma'am." Then he tipped his cap to my mother and strode away with my brother and sister tucked in the pockets of his greatcoat, their mewing to be heard as he climbed the ladder between decks.

It wasn't until I was left with my mother and my brother Moxie that I began to know there was something different about me. Mind you, I had never been above deck, and I had not seen my own reflection yet, so I had no idea how I appeared to others, except through snips and bits of what the sailors said when they came to see us. I had thought myself unique, especially since Melissa seemed to favor me over my brothers and sisters. "Poor tiny Jacob," she would coo. "Such a bitty kitty you are." She would hold me to her and let me sleep in her lap, especially when the roughhousing of my bigger brothers and sisters proved to be too much for me.

My mother seemed to favor me, too. When the sailors came to have their look at us, she would scoot me behind her or wrap herself around me—hiding me from their large hands and rough ways, I thought. But I was almost never handled. The sailors would reach for the largest kitten first, and that was always someone other than I. That is, until it was just me and Moxie left in the basket.

My brother was a funny sort of cat, a bit odd about the face, and with ears too large for his head. He was black and white, with two white paws in front, markings that my father had as well. I learned this from one captain who stopped by. "He's got socks on, like his old man!" he chuckled. "Won't be able to catch mice with those, now, will you?" he asked Moxie, scratching him beneath the chin. Then he turned his eyes to me and said, "Better luck than your brother here, though. A runt, and four white mittens to boot. You'll be lucky to give that one away." As he spoke, my mother's tail began to swish, and her purring stopped. This escaped the notice of the man, though, as he lifted Moxie from the basket and began to talk price with Captain Natick.

I watched the money change hands, and the large man walk away with Moxie, my last sibling. Now it was just me in the basket with Mother. I hadn't given much thought to what might happen to me, but now I did. Would someone come and tuck me into a greatcoat pocket as well—carry me away? I could hardly bear the thought, and I burrowed under Mother's paws to hide. She purred and licked my face, and it occurred to me that her own sadness must outweigh mine. How selfish of me to worry only for myself, when my poor mother had watched, without one mew of complaint, as all of her kittens, save one, had been taken off by strangers.

A light again made its way across the darkness of the galley toward us, and I saw, as it approached, that the captain's long arm held a lantern out before him. I shuddered; this must be it—my time had come. Then I saw that with him was only Melissa. What did this mean for me? If no other captain had claimed me, what was to be my fate?

"Daddy, please, can't we keep Jacob? No one wanted him. And poor Mrs. Tibbs needs to keep just one of her babies. Please, Daddy?"

The captain didn't answer, but continued to hold his lantern out over our basket. My mother looked up, I observed as she licked the tip of my ear just once, but kept her eyes locked on the captain.

"That's what it is to have a mother," said Melissa. "Mrs. Tibbs doesn't care that he's a runt, or that he's got four mittens on." Melissa covered her mouth with a white cloth and coughed again, holding on to her chest. The captain's eyes got that watery look, and I knew then that whatever Melissa wanted, she was bound to get. "She just loves him all the same," Melissa said quietly, kneeling to our basket.

With those words, my fate was sealed. The captain took off his hat, pushed back a lock of fair hair, and came down on one knee. He laid a hand on my mother's head and scratched her roughly behind the ears, as was his style. "Batten down, Mrs. Tibbs. We'll be leaving port in the morning. And it looks as though we'll have a stowaway by the name of Jacob Tibbs on board as well."

CHAPTER 2

A LOADING-TO DAY

In the still-dark dawn of the next morn, my mother woke me with a gentle nudge and a swish of her tail. I clung to my warm spot in our basket until I remembered, all at once, that this was the day we would be leaving port. Until now the whole of my world had been below deck, in our basket in the galley, and I'd made the acquaintance of only a few sailors. But this would be the first day my mother would let me join her topside. I knew it to be an important day, so I roused and gave myself a quick bath.

Mother looked me over, as she did every morning, and tidied up my fur where I'd missed a spot. I noticed that her short yellow-and-white hair, which resembled my own, was all in place. Our markings were nearly identical, save for our paws—where mine were a milky shade of white, mother's were a warm, solid yellow. I thought my mother a very handsome cat, but on this morning she had clearly taken extra care. With her ears perked and her white whiskers straight, the *M* on her high forehead stood out in dark orange. She turned on her back paws and made her way to the ship's pantry. I knew to follow close behind.

Though the sun was not yet up, there was a great deal of fuss and bother going on. Big, loud sailors were everywhere, men I'd never laid eyes on, moving about with parcels large and small. I'd never seen so much activity, and I stopped in my tracks and watched in wonderment. The sailors had formed a line, and each passed a parcel to the man next to him before turning to catch another, and so on, all the way down the galley row and into the pantry—a closet of a room that would store all of our food for the journey we were about to undertake. This line of men went right out the ship through a small hatch at the side, the port door, through which a chill breeze was blowing. The men chanted a kind of song as they moved their goods: "Heave!" one would say as he tossed a bag of flour, "Ho!" the man catching the thrown parcel would call out, and on down the line like that.

The smells that filled the ship were divine: dried meats, fresh breads, bright fruits and vegetables, barrels of salt and sugar, and huge bags of flour. And oh, they had such a way to stow things! Sailors find every nook and cranny in a ship and stash things in places the likes of which you could never imagine. Up high were rows of cupboards, and down low barrels lined the walls. Bags and bins were hung from ceiling hooks and strapped to the inside walls of the ship. Anything that didn't fit into the small pantry was stowed into the galley, wherever space could be found. All the food and drink we would need for our journey was loaded on and stored in this way. It was an amazing scene to behold, and in the confusion I lost sight of my mother. I regret to recount that it did not take me long to find myself in trouble without her.

It all started when one sailor, not noticing, nearly stepped on me in his haste. He stumbled, then looked down on me and called out, "What's this! Mrs. Tibbs, I do believe you've let a scruffy yellow rat in our galley!" I knew the most important part of my mother's job was to see that the rat population on the *Melissa Rae* was kept to a minimum, so she took this kind of comment, even if meant only in jest, very seriously.

In the bustle around us, Mother had moved to the other side of the line of men, and she was now across the pantry from me, hard at work checking the fresh parcels for vermin. She looked up when she heard her name, caught my eye, and in a flash was back beside me. She gently picked me up by the scruff of my neck and carried me between the legs of the large sailors to the other side of the room, where she set me down.

"What's that, Mrs. Tibbs? A wee kitten, do you s'pose, or has she found herself a rat that she fancies?" someone called out.

"Heave!" cried another sailor just over my head. "Ho!" said his mate, setting down a huge bag of flour so close to me that the boards under my four paws rattled, and I was coated entirely from head to tail in a layer of white flour dust. And if that wasn't enough, I took to a sneezing fit the likes of which I'd never known.

"My lands! He's covered in dust. Looks like a ghost of a rat now, he does!" There was a hearty laugh to be heard up and down the line as I sneezed again and shook myself best I could. Quick as you please, my mother returned to my side, and I could tell she was far from happy with my appearance—or with the comments of the sailors. Knowing now what I do about the urgency of a loading-to day, it's a wonder she didn't take me topside and toss me overboard just to have me out from underfoot. Instead she gently picked me up again and leapt from bag to bag until she could drop me atop a tall barrel, and there she left me. From this vantage point I could watch my mother do her work, and I was out of the way of the busy sailors.

And watch I did. The bags were being tossed at such a speed over my head that I began to know my first seasickness—this before we'd even put out to sea! I peered over the edge of the barrel to see where my mother had gone, but I'd again lost sight of her in all the furious activity of the sailors.

Searching over the other side of the barrel, I still had no sign of her. Perhaps being on this barrel wasn't in my favor after all. But my legs were too small to get me safely down. I mewed once, softly, calling my mother, hoping she would hear me. The draft from the open port door blew hard just then and sent flour dust stirring up. After another sneezing fit, I ran to the other side of the barrel and cried again for my mother. Where was she? I'd almost never been apart from her. Had she left me here for good? How would I ever get down? I closed my eyes tight and let out my loudest cry, meowing over and over, hoping it would cut through the din and send my mother back to me.

"Ah, that racket's got to be stopped," said one sailor as he dropped his parcel and wiped his brow. "I've enough of an 'eadache without this one starting in. Where's your Mrs. Tibbs got herself?" I stopped crying for a moment as the sailor approached me. "Even an old salt as me knows what it is to want your mum." His warm hand closed around me, and he brought me up to his chest. I looked into his face and saw that his eyes were a very warm brown color. His face was tanned and freckled and crossed with deep lines, and he had a bushy red beard—in fact, it was the first time I'd seen that much hair on a person! His colors reminded me of Butterscotch, and I instantly liked him.

"Throw that rat into the cupboard, Sean, and let's get back to work," a big sailor standing behind him said roughly.

"Naw, now, you know one of Mrs. Tibbs's needs to be treated well, mate," said the red-bearded sailor.

Another sailor, a boy who seemed not much bigger than Melissa, came up alongside and petted my head gently. "Just a little scrub, he is." He touched my paws and tried to rub the flour dust off them. "By gum, come have a look, Chippy. He's got little white paws, every one."

The big sailor, called Chippy, finally dropped his work

and huffed over. "Means he won't be any good to us this trip out, nor any other." He looked down at me, and I up at him. The dark patch he wore over one eye and his deep booming voice made a terrifying combination. He shook his head. "That's the type that can't catch a rat t'save his life."

His mate with the red beard looked at him skeptically. "What's that, just because he has white paws?"

Chippy nodded. "Those white paws are a sign that a cat won't be a good mouser. Rats can see those paws in the dark of the hold, coming close, and they skitter away. This one has all four." He rubbed my paw roughly in his fingers. "And mitts soft as silk! Should just toss him overboard now."

"Mrs. T. isn't as young as she used to be. D'ya think the captain wants to replace her with this one?" the young sailor asked.

The red-bearded sailor holding me perked up. "Shhh, don't talk such nonsense, Daly. And you, too, Chippy. It's bad luck to speak ill of the cap's cat, you both know that. If anything untoward happens on this journey, I'll be holding you the guilty parties."

Just then, a fat face poked down the open hatch. "Eh, what's the holdup, fellows?" the man asked. "The good cap'n wants to know if we'll be ready loaded by eight bells. Shall I inform him that I've seen nothing but lagging about and little work, or will you bother to get on with it?" With that the sailors all scrabbled back to their posts and picked up their dropped parcels. The sailor named Chippy glanced up at the open hatch, as if to be sure the fat-faced fellow was gone before speaking. "Between our new first mate Archer and havin' that rat on board, I believe this trip'll be the death of me."

The man called Sean who held me in his hands smiled at me again with his warm brown eyes and whispered, "Archer may be a rat, but you're surely not. Stay put, and we'll not have more talk like that." With one swift motion he tucked me deep into his wide jacket pocket.

Though I still wondered after my mother—and felt sorry for getting all the sailors in trouble with the first mate—I was grateful for the warm, cozy pocket I found myself in. I could hear the sounds of the men chanting their working song around me, a bit louder now, perhaps (for the benefit of anyone listening, I suppose). I must have closed my eyes and drifted off, for the next I knew, I was above deck for the very first time.

CHAPTER 3

MILK-AND-WATER SEAS

When I awoke, it was to the feel of a great hand closing around my middle. I was pulled from the sailor's pocket and plopped, rather unceremoniously, on the deck of the ship. I spotted my mother nearby, but she took almost no notice of me. She was sniffing the air and swishing her tail in an agitated way.

"There you are, Mrs. Tibbs," the sailor said, nudging me gently with his boot. "Here's what you've been looking for." I was still a bit sleepy from my nap, but even I could tell that Mother wasn't concerned for me. There seemed to be something else on her mind. But she did pick me up by the scruff of my neck and carry me up a small set of stairs to the front part of the ship, putting me down on what I would soon learn was called the forecastle deck. From there I found myself looking over the bow for the very first time.

As we were in port, the *Melissa Rae* was tied fast to the

dock, but I could still see a great body of water around us. It was huge, stretching out as far as the eye could see. When I looked up, I'd never seen anything bigger than the sky that day as the sun burst forth. The water below was dark and looked quite solid to me until a breeze gently rippled the surface. I was amazed by the way it moved as it waved and slapped the side of the ship with a soothing *clunk, clunk, clunk.* I had heard that sound below deck, too, but now I saw the source and how great the ocean was around us.

My mother gave me a once-over and seemed very disappointed. I suppose I was still a bit covered in flour dust, and my nap in the close quarters of the sailor's pocket probably hadn't done my fur any favors. But Mother took the time to clean me off and straighten my whiskers. When she was done, she sat back and gave me another look. This time the sparkle in her eye told me she was again ready to have me at her side.

She turned, twitched her tail quickly, and led me forward along the forecastle deck. There Captain Natick stood in his full uniform. I'd never seen him dressed up, and I took in his new appearance with great awe. He wore a suit of navy with gold medals pinned to the chest and lapels. Beneath the jacket was a crisp white shirt, and on his shoulders were strips of gold fabric with tassels that dangled and swung when he moved. They looked like great fun, and I eyed them curiously, wishing to be brought up near his shoulders to see if I could catch one with my paws. Mother stopped near the captain's feet and mewed. "Ah, Mrs. Tibbs," the captain greeted us, looking down. "I'm glad both you and Jacob are here to see us off. We're started a bit later in the morning than expected, but still, the sea looks pleasant, does it not?"

When I turned back to my mother, she stood proud with her head held high and her chin up. She was looking not down into the dark glittering ocean as I was, but straight out at the vast horizon that lay before us, with one paw poised in front of the other. In all the days I've set out to sea since then, I've always remembered that moment, watching my mother at her post, as if commanding the ship herself. She was a regal cat, and I'm sure I'll never know her equal on sea or land.

Just then a bell rang, and I heard a voice call out, "All hands!" Immediately the sailors hurried forth. They had been looking over the port side of the ship, waving goodbye to friends and family, but now took up the serious work of setting us to sea. There was a great flapping sound as the sails were drawn up their poles and the sailors called out to one another. I watched the huge white triangles of cloth go up and up and up . . . The masts were so tall, I could barely see the tops. In all, three huge sails were heaved up, bit by bit, hauled by ropes that the men held down on deck. When the sails were as high and as tight as they wanted them to be, they tied off the great ropes. I left my mother at the bow and wandered over to investigate the knots—which were many times as big around as my whole self!

The air on deck was nothing like the warmth down below. As I made my way across the deck, I noticed that the sea breeze was chilled so that it almost hurt to breathe it in. The smell was a little different, too—strong and salty, not like the sweet smell of my mother's basket or the food smells I knew from the galley. The ropes, when I reached them, smelled of salt, too, and of a woodsy resin—the tar and wax the sailors had used to hold them together. Sniffing at the thick mast that held the knotted twine, I decided it was a good time to sharpen my claws a bit, and I set my front paws into the wood. I dug hard two or three times, feeling quite grown up about things, before hands scooped me up.

"Jacob, I'll not have you tearing at my ship," said the captain. "Now, why can't you stay by your mum and have a look at how she does her job?" Being so close to the tassels on his uniform, I heard very little of what the captain was saying and instead couldn't resist taking a whap at the golden strings to see what would happen. The captain said nothing as he held me out from his chest. His ice-blue eyes met mine, and when he spoke, his voice had a serious tone. "This day is not for playing. Run along to your mother, and stay put." Then he plopped me down and straightened out the tassels on his shoulder, shaking his head as a small smile crossed his lips.

My mother was close by, still standing at the bow of the ship and staring out to sea. I took a spot beside her and watched as the sailors pulled up the huge ropes that held us fast to the dock. They coiled them in great loops on either side of the deck. I wanted to see more but was afraid to leave my mother's side again in all the activity.

Standing as I was, so close to my mother, I caught sight of her as she did something that seemed quite odd. She tipped her head back and sniffed the sea air, first to her right, then to her left. Then, with one paw, she gently scratched the deck three times, smoothly drawing her claws back: one, two, three.

I was puzzled, as I'd never seen my mother act this way. She seemed to be in a trance, staring out at the sea, and her eyes held the horizon as if nothing could tear her away. She did not break her concentration, even as I nudged her side. So rapt was I with studying my mother that I took no notice of the captain as he came up alongside us. But my mother must have sensed him there, and again she scratched at the deck three times, pulling her paw back slowly and deliberately each time, just as she had done before.

The captain knelt down and stroked her back. "What's this, then? You and Jacob have both taken a fancy to scratching up my boat?"

My mother did not falter, and with the captain's hand still on her back, she scratched the deck three more times—this time even more slowly and exactly.

"Ah, rough weather, is it?" the captain asked my mother quietly. He looked out over the sea, studying the horizon for a moment. I did not know what his eyes were searching for, but he seemed not to find it. "Jacob," he said, turning to me, "that's the sign your mother makes when she smells rough weather ahead. But pay you no mind today. All the reports are favorable. I think our Mrs. Tibbs has perhaps grown a little too cautious in her old age, haven't you, luv? You've not been yourself since this last litter."

He smoothed her fur and went on. "The sea's as smooth as a looking glass, Mrs. Tibbs, and I'm promised to reach New York in about forty days' time. We sat out the last storm, but I can't afford to wait another day in port." With his petting, my mother finally broke her gaze and turned to meet his eyes. She looked worried, I think, but she bowed her head and allowed him to scratch behind her ears.

The captain stood up and held fast to the taut rope that ran just below the forward sail, looking out over the sea. What a picture they made, him turned out in his navy suit, my mother in her regal pose. I suddenly felt the overwhelming task that lay before them—before all of us, really, as I was also to be a part of this great adventure. It was no small feat to cross the Atlantic with a hold full of goods, a ship full of men, and to safely reach land on the other side. I tried to strike the pose my mother was in, and held my head high, though the shifting of the ship made it difficult to stand still for long.

"Milk-and-water seas, Captain," I heard Sean call out from behind us as he heaved the rope on board. "It'll be smooth as silk."

The sailor's words snapped the captain back to attention. "Aye there, Sean," he replied, then he added, quietly, as if to himself, "And we'll all be home again soon, safe as houses, and back with my dear girl, Melissa."

If the captain's words sounded a little uncertain, I felt no fear. Instead, at the mention of her name, I only longed to see Melissa, her gentle hands and soothing voice, though I knew she wouldn't be allowed on board today, nor anywhere near the ship. The captain was, if nothing else, a superstitious man, and he strongly believed that women could only bring ill fortune to a seagoing vessel. Why this rule seemed not to apply to cats, I never did know—for my own mother was a lady and never was seen to bring anything but the best of luck to the *Melissa Rae*. At least until this, her last voyage. But that is a story long in the telling.

CHAPTER 4

A STORM BREWS

When we actually set sail, leaving Liverpool far behind, it was not the momentous occasion I thought it would be. We pulled away from the dock, with no more slosh or sway than when we'd been moored, and the ship moved out to sea. I watched as the boards of the great dock slipped into one big brown line behind us, and then as the entire wharf turned into a thin sliver on the horizon. Before long the sight of land was lost altogether, and all that lay in front of us was more and more sea.

Since I'd never known life away from the *Melissa Rae*, it didn't strike me as odd to be surrounded by nothing but water—I still felt at home. But the movement of the ship was new. We were constantly in motion, always going forward and pitching as the ship rocked and swayed from side to side.

There was one among the sailors, the fat-faced fellow called Archer, who seemed unwell from the moment we left port. When he had yelled at the sailors to hurry their work when they were loading to, I had seen only his round, ruddy face looking down from the open hatch, but now I could take in the rest of him, and I was not impressed: He was a short man with a high, round belly that pushed against his jacket buttons. As the *Melissa Rae* took to the sea, he spent a good amount of time with his head over the side of the ship, food coming out of his mouth instead of going in it, until his usually blotchy face was decidedly green in color. This was before I knew what seasickness was, and I foolishly assumed that perhaps he had a hairball, as my mother sometimes did, for that made her cough and retch as Archer was doing. As for myself, I did not feel unwell, but I will admit it was hard to line up one paw in front of the other as I paced the deck of the ship. The sailors were still hard at work, and I tried my best to stay from beneath their feet. And when I did happen to tumble, I was ashamed to have anyone else as witness—especially the cruel ones among the crew.

"Look at the wee kitty have a go on his sea legs!" hollered out the sailor with the black eye patch, whom I recognized as Chippy. "Can't go five paces without the wind blowing 'im over!" The other sailors watched as I tried desperately to stay upright and cross the deck at the same time. But as the wind kicked up, it set the ship and me swaying with it. My paws would step down where the ship planks were supposed to be, and the ground would surely move from beneath me. After nearly getting splinters along my whole self, I ended up standing beside one of the great masts, my claws dug into the deck to hold me anchored, until I caught sight of my mother.

Unbelievably, she was scurrying, paw over paw, down the ratlines of the ship. How had she gotten up there? I wondered. The ratlines were ropes tied together in such a way as to form a ladder for the sailors to reach the sails. Set, as they were, in squares at least a foot between and not much wider across, they were hard even for the sailors to travel. Yet there was my mother, Mrs. Tibbs, stepping just as daintily as you please from rope to rope as she made her way to the deck. When her paws touched the solid wood again, I noticed that her once-orderly fur had gotten ruffled, and that her ears were turned up to the sky, as if in tune to every sound. Her eyes were startling—so green, with only a tiny dark slit of black in the middle. She looked at me to check that I was faring all right, and then, quick, she was off across the deck. I watched in awe as she made her way at a steady gait even with the tossing of the ship.

She wove around the sailors' moving feet like she was in a maze that she'd learned by heart. She seemed to know, expertly, who would step where next, and just how the ship would pitch, and she would make allowance for it in her path. The sailors, for their part, seemed to take no notice of her, and there was no laughter about Mrs. Tibbs's sea legs. She made it look so easy that I decided to follow her example and find out, in the process, just where she was off to in such a rush. So I loosened my claws from where they were anchored and walked a few paces. But I was timid of the sailors' footfalls, and of the ship's great to and fro. How was it that my mother could make such short work of this? Ashamed, but with no other option, I slowly made my way to the bulwark wall that lined the deck and kept my right side steady to it as I scurried, scared as a tiny mouse, to the back of the ship.

When I reached the quarterdeck, near the captain's cabin, without catching another glimpse of my mother, I assumed there was only one place she could be. A quick sniff at the door to the captain's quarters told me that she had just been there, so I set to mewing and scratching at the door. Oh, what a nuisance I made of myself! I'm ashamed to recall how I behaved those first days out, just like the infant I was. But my noises worked, and it wasn't long before the door was pulled open and I made my way into the darkness that lay within. I noticed at once that the room smelled like Melissa—of starched freshness and clean linens, and lemon-drop candy. Melissa was on board! I thought with glee.

But as I searched the quarters, I did not happen on her face. Only the captain was there, with his first mate, Archer, and of course my mother. Where was Melissa? I paced, my paws taking in the softness of the woven rug that lined the floor, and finally found my Melissa upon the wall . . . but it wasn't really her. Instead it was only her face, flat and unmoving, set in a great gold frame on one wall above a shelf of books. And there was a woman with her, someone who looked just like Melissa, except that her blond hair was all piled up on her head and held there with a wide blue ribbon. And the woman wasn't smiling like Melissa; she was staring straight out into the room, as if she were looking at someone. I stopped dead in my tracks and stared back at the blond woman and at Melissa, too. *What a strange thing,* I thought, *to have a pretend Melissa here in this room!*

I quickly took in the rest of the quarters. It was a grand place, with all manner of lovely things. There was a set of stuffed and fluffy chairs that looked like a very nice place to curl up for a nap and a cozy small bed that was built along one wall. Toward the front of the cabin was a great wooden desk with paper slips and instruments piled on top. There was the picture of Melissa and the woman, who I presumed to be her mother, on one wall, and along the other wall was a picture of a big swath of green and a big blue sky. I'd never set foot on grass in my life, so it took me some time to know what that picture was. On this, my first sighting, it looked to be a big green square topped by a big blue square, with a little redbrick house on the horizon. It was puzzling to me, but I assumed the captain must like it for some reason and like it well enough to hang it in his quarters with a portrait of Melissa.

The captain picked me up and held me in the crook of his arm, adding a nice scratch under my chin as he resumed a conversation with his first mate. "I know to the eye it's clear, but this cat of mine has not been wrong once in her nine lives. Something has her on, and I'll wager there's a storm brewing." I noted then that my mother was pacing upon the captain's desk and looking out the small window above it. I couldn't believe that the captain would allow her to step across his papers and maps but he didn't seem to mind. She pawed at the desk, pushing important-looking documents around, then stopped to glance out at the sea.

Archer coughed into a handkerchief, his face still pale from his latest bout of seasickness. "Sir, pardon me for breathing it out loud, but your cat here has seen better times. How long has he been with you? Ten years or more?"

The captain quickly corrected him, without directly answering his insult to my mother's abilities. "*Her* name is Mrs. Tibbs, and this is her young one, Jacob."

Archer petted my head with a thick hand and sent a wave of fear through me. There was something about him I didn't like, and it was more than the words he'd spoken about my mother—and in her presence, no less, the cheek of him! He was insincere, and yet I could tell he was worried as well. But why didn't he speak his mind?

"Perhaps we should batten down, just in case . . ." As the captain spoke, my mother pushed—by accident or by design—a metal tool off the desk, and it hit the floor with a loud thunk. Both men stopped and turned to look.

Quickly Archer picked up the metal triangle. "Captain, I hesitate to mention this, but I have been made aware of your sad fortune: the recent passing of your wife, and your child ill with the same—"

The captain's face was stern as he cut off the other man

midsentence. "What business is my family to do with you or your command of this ship?"

"Ah, but it is business indeed, Captain. Please, hear me out." Archer turned and folded his arms behind his back, pacing the cabin, before continuing. "It is only this: that I would not want to see your vessel, named for your beloved daughter, make poor time crossing and miss a bonus that awaits us all in New York. Imagine what good an extra wage would do for your child's care and medicines. Not to mention the reputation of the *Melissa Rae*."

As he spoke, I watched the captain's face soften, and he began to nod.

"And of course, none of us want to spend too long away from our loved ones. A quick crossing is welcome to all—not only those with a sickly child back in port."

The captain put me down upon his desk, right next to my mother, who took to licking my ears and face with her rough tongue. "Perhaps you're right," the captain said. "Mrs. Tibbs can be a bit odd after passing a litter." My mother seemed not to hear his words, but she did stop her cleaning and glanced out the starboard window, still watching the sky. "We'll need to catch every bit of this wind to make our time," the captain finished, putting his hand out for my mother to come closer.

The first mate looked on as the captain scratched my mother's chin, and, if possible, he went a bit greener about the gills. He seemed to be sickened by the captain's affections for us. Perhaps it was just the pitch of the ship affecting his stomach again. "Shall I give the order, then, sir?" Archer asked, breaking the spell that seemed to surround the four of us.

"Yes, Mr. Archer. You may give the order," the captain replied.

As Archer made for the door, my mother hopped down from the desk to follow him, and I was quick on her tail. This must be some sort of official ship business that called for the presence of the ship's cat, and I did not want to miss a moment of it, despite the lure of a possible nap in the soft chairs of the captain's quarters.

We left the captain behind and trailed Archer as he stepped out and made his way toward the steps leading down to the main deck. But instead of stepping down, he stood on the edge of the quarterdeck and called to a sailor below him. "You there," he said. "Ring for all hands—I've got word from the captain."

I recognized the sailor at once. He was the brown-eyed, red-bearded fellow called Sean who had secured me in his pocket as we loaded to. Sean looked up at Mr. Archer now and answered curtly, "Not for me to do, sir. That's Chippy MacNeil's job, to do the ringing. He'll have my hide or yours if we touch his bell."

"Fine, then, would you bring this Mr. MacNeil to me so that I may give him the order?" Archer spat out.

"I would, sir, but he was on the morning and the forenoon watch and is asleep in his bunk now."

"Well, then, who's to ring the bell if he's asleep—I mean, surely someone else can ring the bell?" Archer was getting flustered now, and turning quite red in the face and all down his neck.

"You won't find a sailor aboard who's willing to suffer Chippy's rage. You'd best just step down here and ring it yourself."

"I will not!" Archer squealed. "I've got orders from the captain, and you will ring that bell this instant!"

I could tell from the way Sean's brown eyes got all crinkly that he was trying terribly hard not to laugh at poor Mr. Archer.

"I tell you, sir, I cannot, and what's more, I won't," Sean said, and turned his back on us, returning to his work. The other sailors around him pretended not to hear the exchange, but I could tell they all had, and were quietly laughing to themselves as they ducked their heads and went about their jobs.

Just then the captain came around the quarterdeck. "Orders given?" he asked.

"Not just quite, sir," Archer answered, trying to hold down his temper. "It appears that only one man aboard is able to ring for all hands, and that man's asleep in his bunk at the moment."

"Well, that hardly matters," the captain pointed out, "as all hands will call him up, and he's bound to be awake for that." There was a glint in the captain's eye as he took the steps to the main deck. "In that case, you just have to ring the bell yourself. I'm sure you can manage that. Here, I'll show you how." The captain rang the bell three times, calling out deeply, "All hands!"

Then he came back up the steps and said to Archer, "I'll leave you to it?"

Archer, his face and neck now gone crimson, murmured an angry "Yes, sir," as the captain strolled by.

"Then I'll be in my cabin," the captain said with a little grin, "should you find that you need me."

CHAPTER 5

RED SKY BY MORNING

As the sailors lined up just below the quarterdeck, Archer let out a loud sneeze. And another. And another. "Ah-*choo*," he sneezed one last time, then swatted his handkerchief toward my mother, who was sitting beside his feet. "Go on then, you disgusting creature! Get off," he sputtered.

My mother jumped out of the way just as Archer kicked at her, his boot barely missing her side. A low growl escaped her throat—the first time I'd ever heard her make that noise—and she picked me up by my scruff, carrying me down the steps to where the sailors stood. I couldn't help but wonder if perhaps Archer had gotten a bit of loose flour up his nose, as I had had the misfortune to suffer through a similar fit of sneezing that very morning. I puzzled over his intense dislike for us as Mother and I quickly slid into the crowd. All attention was back on Archer as he finally cleared his throat to give the orders.

"Right, then . . . ah . . . ," Archer started. He crossed his arms over his ample belly and looked out at the men blankly.

"You'll be wanting our names, sir?" suggested one sailor.

"Yes, that's it. State your names!" said Archer boldly, as if he had thought of it himself.

The sailors fell into a rather rumpled line and started calling off:

"Sean Reid, sir, second mate," called out Sean as he gave Archer a grin from under his bushy red beard.

"Charles MacNeil," growled the surly sailor with the eye patch whom I knew to be called Chippy. "Third mate, ship's carpenter," he added with another grumble.

"Douglas Dougherty," said the next sailor, a giant of a man with black muttonchop whiskers as large as my whole self.

"Smyth, sir, John Smyth," whistled out the tall blond fellow next to him, but the way he said it, it sounded more like "Shh-myth, shir." This lanky sailor had teeth like piano keys, with big spaces between. When he talked, the air whistled through his mouth, giving certain words a *sh* sound. The other sailors teased him a bit, but I later learned he was a vicious cardsharp, so I suppose they didn't laugh for long when they lost a week's wages to him in a card game.

"Slattery," called out a young redheaded sailor, and on it went down the line, each sailor calling out his name.

"Moses, ship's cook," called out a fellow that I'd not seen before. He was very small and could not have weighed much more than Melissa. His head was empty of hair and gleamed like well-polished brass in the bright sun. He stood in an odd way, as if leaning forward, and I realized all at once that he had only one leg. Where his other leg should have been was a thick stick of wood that vanished into his trousers. His arms, which were bare to the elbow, were tanned and covered in marks and letters and drawings of all sorts of things—anchors and boats, even a lady with a fish tail! He looked down at me and winked when he caught me staring up at him. I glanced away, embarrassed to have been caught, and scooted under my mother's legs.

Archer clasped his hands behind his back and began to pacc thc little space of the quarterdeck. "I've been sent with orders from the captain. All sails up, and at full mast. We're to make good use of this wind while it lasts." Archer stopped pacing and looked at the men.

"So you'll be wanting all hands until the second dog, sir?" Sean asked.

"Er, second dog . . ." Archer furrowed his brows in thought.

"That would be the last evening watch, sir, from six hours to eight hours past noon bell."

"Yes. Second dogwatch. All hands until then. Good." Archer nodded and turned on his heel.

"Sir, if I may," Chippy rumbled, his voice a raspy growl.

"There's been some talk that this strong wind means poor weather. And we had a touch of red sky by morning. Is it wise, you think, to open full sails?"

Archer took a deep breath. "The captain has passed these orders. If you doubt them based on an old wives' tale, or, worse yet, on the temperament of a silly sea cat, then you are hardly fit to be on this ship. The captain's orders remain, and will be executed as given." Again Archer turned to leave.

Sean cleared his throat loudly and spoke up. "If you're through, you'll be wanting to dismiss us, Mr. Archer, sir." There were a few snickered laughs among the other sailors.

Archer glanced back, looking humbled. "Indeed, and I was just getting to that." He turned and faced the men, setting his heels together and sticking out his round belly. "Dismissed!" he yelled, looking more flustered by the minute. This time he practically ran back to the captain's cabin. And no sooner had he closed the door behind him than the sailors all burst into raucous laughter.

"If he's not heaving his insides out, he's giving orders, then, is he?" Chippy said with a deep laugh. "If not for his father, he'd never have set foot on board the good Captain Natick's ship."

"His father buys the shipping company, and shuddenly his shon is fit to be our firsht mate," Smyth added, with his funny way of talking. "And him calling ush 'not fit to be on board' indeed! I've not heard shuch wash in ages!"

"Did you see him this morning, with his head over the

side, gasping and spewing? On me mum's good name, I'd swear he's never been aboard before in his life!" Dougherty roared.

Sean did not join in their laughter; instead he stood looking out over the sea. "Mates," he said quietly, "much as we doubt and distrust this Archer fellow, the issue remains: Captain did give those orders. Are we to carry them out, or no?"

"Aye, but the cap gave those orders *because* of Archer—we've got to make our best time across, for fear he'll report back to his father otherwise," the red-haired sailor called Slattery answered.

The cook, Moses, knelt to my mother's side and ran his hand down her back as she purred her greeting to him. "I've sailed with this lady for more years than I care to recall. And in all that time, she's been wrong never. I say we listen to Mrs. Tibbs—this Mr. Archer be damned!"

"Hear, hear!" said Slattery, and the other sailors called out their agreement.

But Sean spoke up again. "As a free man, I'm agreeing with you. But as second mate, you know I've got to ask that you fulfill the good captain's orders, even if they be delivered to us by an unseaworthy imbecile." He paused and gave the sailors a moment to laugh. "So I propose this: We'll put to full sails, but we'll be on the ready for anything. We've run this ship through a good bit of weather in our time, and we can see her battened down in a half bell if there's trouble to be had. Is there any among you who would call me wrong?" Sean looked to the men standing around him. Their faces were grim, but no one spoke up. "Then it's orders as given, and all hands ready until second dog."

"Aye," said Chippy.

"Aye," answered Moses. The other sailors chimed in, and in no time the deck was busy with the scrabbling sailors, again hard at work.

Everywhere I looked, large white sails were billowing, and sailors were calling out orders or singing group songs as they did their duties tying off ropes and pulling up the heavy canvases. I watched as my mother resumed her post at the bow of the ship, and I toddled after her, trying to make my way through the sailors' quick-moving feet, the lashing ropes, and the sweeping wind.

When I reached her side, she stood as she had before, trancelike, near the dangling anchor. I would soon learn that the angled piece of wood where the anchor was stowed was called the cathead—a fitting name, as it was situated at the bow and made a perfect lookout for agile sea cats. As Mother stared out to sea, I took my place beside her and tried to see what she saw in the line of the horizon. What was she looking at? To me it appeared nothing but water and wind and sky. Then, all at once, a feeling came over me. It is hard to put into words, harder than most feelings because it is not an emotion like "sad" or "happy" or "scared."

Instead it started in my paws, like a little tickle. Then a vibration that traveled up my legs and seemed to settle in my chest. My heart beat faster as I stared out over the ocean. I felt my ears hum, and around me the noise and activity of the sailors slipped away without my notice. My fear of the trembling ship left me as well, for I was suddenly sturdy on my legs and felt them lock into place, my head held high. In my mind one thing took focus, one thought that I knew without doubt—something was waiting for us, just beyond the sunlight, just beyond the day. Something wicked was waiting for us, and with our sails full up, we were now rushing to meet it.

CHAPTER 6

THE BEGINNING OF THE END

The storm came from nowhere, or so it seemed to the men on board. But to me, and to my mother, it came on slow, and the agony of waiting for it is perhaps the most punishing feeling a true ship's cat can have.

The sails were full up and the sky was clear when the bells were rung eight, signaling the end of the afternoon watch and the start of the evening. I didn't know ship's clock just yet, as this was my first time out, but I did know that most hands had been on deck since we'd left port many hours before. This meant that not many sailors had had a bit of rest, or a bite of food, since sunrise. The men were tired, and longed for the four bells that would signal the end of first dogwatch. At that, half the men on deck could go below for rest and a drink of water, and maybe Moses, the cook, would grub up some food. The other sailors, though, would stay on deck for second dog, another two hours, until the night watch, when their rest would begin.

It was still a bit before sunset when the sky took dark. It did not grow dim, as normal twilight does. Instead the shade moved across the deck, like an eclipse, from port to starboard, crawling up the ship. And with the darkness came even stronger winds. The sails had been full all day, but this was a change, blowing hard, steady, and showing no sign of letting. The captain was out of his cabin before the sun was off the bowsprit. "Aye, why was I not told about this change in the weather?" he snapped at Mr. Archer.

"'Tis just come up out of nowhere, sir," said Archer, looking at the dark sky. "I've never seen anything like it."

"You've never seen the like as you've never been aboard a ship at sea," the captain said harshly. This was the first time I'd heard him use a rough tone to anyone, and it scared me from my wits. He quickly went on: "But I have seen the like of this, and these men have as well." The captain motioned to the sailors on deck. Every man had dropped his work, and all were staring at the ominous sky as if in shock.

"Our Lord," I heard the big man called Dougherty say. "It's a storm of the Devil, it is." He stroked his muttonchop whiskers and stared up at the dark sky.

"Don't you say it, Dougie," the red-haired fellow called Slattery begged. "Don't you say that; you'll make it so."

Chippy stepped up to where the captain stood and

whispered, "Is it, sir? Is it Devil's Storm?" His raspy voice was as soft as I'd ever heard it.

The captain did not answer him, nor look at him. "Ring for all hands, Mr. MacNeil. And bring Mrs. Tibbs to me, when you find her."

Chippy ran to the bell and rang hard. "All hands! All hands!" he hollered. But his strong, deep voice didn't need to carry too far; the men were already lining up in the growing darkness that seemed to cover the ship entirely. Chippy came alongside my mother and me where we stood by the cathead of the ship. He scooped my mother up quick and started back to the captain, leaving me behind. I watched his back as he made his way across the deck, and I crouched low, my belly on the deck, cowering, scared to be alone. I could feel what was coming, just as my mother had hours and hours ago, and I cursed the feeling. It was terrible to know, being powerless to stop it.

"I won't have any talk of Devil's Storm on this ship," the captain began, addressing the men. "This is no more than a summer thunder. Mrs. Tibbs here"—he motioned to my mother as she was let down by Chippy—"she gave warning, and I chose, unwisely, to ignore both her and the high winds as we set out. So let's not have such talk; you all know it to be bad luck."

The sailors stayed silent and in line, their eyes on the captain. I couldn't tell from watching their backs if they believed him or not. This was the first I'd heard of Devil's Storm, but I have learned since that it is the worst type of sea storm one can encounter. It comes without any advance warning, and little is known of it, as not one, man or cat, has ever survived its fury. Said to be a storm that the Devil uses for travel, it comes and goes, destroying all unfortunate enough to be in its wake. It never touches land, only sea and the men and ships that sail her.

"We've barely time for sails down," the captain went on. "All hands aloft, the foreyard down, before she strikes. Clear what you can; batten what you cannot. All hands aloft!" With that the captain turned to Archer and ordered, "Bring me my glass."

Archer scrambled into the captain's quarters and brought out a long metal tube, which the captain took and put up to his eye, looking out over the sea. He brought the glass down quickly and pursed his lips, giving a quick whistle in three short bursts. My mother came to attention at his side when he did this, but I was ignorant to the call. I would soon learn, as the captain sighed and said, "Mr. MacNeil, bring Mrs. Tibbs her Jacob, where he stands." Then he put the glass back to his eye and stared out again.

I felt Chippy's hand close around me, hard, and I was lifted. "When the captain whistles, you come, rat. Oh, you'll be the death of me," he hissed as he roughly jostled me across the deck and fairly tossed me at my mother's feet before he turned back to the men on deck.

The sailors raced about, readying the ship, while seconds became minutes and the darkness grew deeper around us. Then from the black sky came cold bits of rain like needles. The captain stood still and held out his hand to catch the drops. Then he did a most unlikely thing—he put his palm up to his mouth and licked the drops. He stood a moment longer and then smiled. "We'll pass through her, men!" he hollered out.

The men above him chanted "Aye, sir!" in return.

Archer watched the captain, obviously as mystified as I.

"I'm looking for a taste of salt." The captain turned to Archer. "If the rain tastes of brine, then we've real trouble. That's salt torn from the sea, and means a hurricane, or worse. But this rain is sweet; 'tis from land. A storm has no mind as to where its rain is from, but to a sailor and his ship it makes all the difference. She'll blow hard, but this storm will run herself out before she takes the *Melissa Rae* with her."

"And putting the rain on your tongue can tell you all that?" Archer scoffed. "Captain, I highly doubt—"

"I am full up with your opinions at the moment, Mr. Archer, so I'll kindly ask you to hold your lip. Your father and his company's desires have put us in this predicament. Now, if you share his passion for profit, you'll set to work with the men and put this vessel in good order."

With that the captain jumped from the quarterdeck and joined his men on the main deck. His glass collapsed into a tidy small tube, which he tucked in his pocket as he took on the rope with Sean and the red-haired boy. All the men were on the main deck, even the one-legged cook, Moses. How they could see around one another, I know not, for it was now pitch-black on deck, and my mother and I had perhaps the best vision of all. I turned to my mother beside me, but her spot was empty. She had followed the captain onto the main deck instead, determined to do her part, I suppose, to help the *Melissa Rae.*

Now the rain began to come on hard, and the punishing drops flew from the sky at such an angle it was almost sideways. I did not care for the feeling of it on my fur; it was cold, and I'd never had the sensation of being entirely wet. In just a few moments, I was in a most uncomfortable state, only made worse by the pitching of the ship. Fairly tossed from side to side, I found myself sliding across the wet deck. With nothing to cling to, I tucked in beside the captain's cabin for safekeeping, and I watched as the youngest boys shimmied up the foremast and ratlines. There was no time for hauling up the wet sails, as the captain said. The four large sails at the front of the ship would need to be cut down. I could see the red-haired boy called Slattery making his way up, his arms and legs wound round the mast, holding on for dear life.

It was then that I heard, for the first time, a noise that I have since come to know—and to fear—well. Over the sound of the rising wind I heard a crying, like a little baby wailing. It took me a moment to recognize what the sound was—the ship's metal fastenings crying out, pulling away from the wood. The high-pitched sound cut through the harsh slashing of the falling rain, and with it came the noise of the ship herself, her wood groaning from high

atop the masts. Between the wailing of the metal and the sickening creak of the ship and the winds, the sailors had to yell to one another to be heard.

I'm not proud to admit it, but I will report this as true. I cowered where I stood, tucked by the captain's cabin at the stern, and watched and listened in terror. I cried for my mother, over and over again, my own ears deaf to my tiny mews under the noise of the storm and the ship. One might think I should be easily forgiven, for this was my first time at sea, and my first storm. I wish I could agree, but the events of that night are not easily forgotten, and I will always question how I behaved. Even now, the scream of the wood and metal and the sounds of that storm on the *Melissa Rae* still haunt me, and I wonder what might have been.

CHAPTER 7

CAT'S EYE

"Lash me in!" I heard the captain holler. From my hiding place I watched as Chippy and Sean wound a thick rope around his waist where he stood at the large wooden wheel behind the quarterdeck. "I'll need someone to be my eyes—send back Mr. Slattery!" the captain yelled to the men as they tied off the rope.

The captain now stood fast, his hands tied to the wheel that steered the *Melissa Rae,* his torso tied, too. Without the strong ropes to bind him, he couldn't possibly have steered the ship—he would have been tossed to the deck, or off the stern altogether, leaving the wheel to spin out of control, damning the ship and her crew to the mercy of the waves wherever the storm would take her.

It looked quite barbaric to me, being tied to the wheel, but I later learned it was common practice during a storm, not just for Captain Natick but for all sea captains. This was why so many captains went down with their ships, because they were literally tied to them—unable to get away even if they did so desire.

The two men left the captain there, ran past where I hid, and leapt onto the main deck. They collected Slattery, who was suffering badly from a fall, and carried him up to the captain. The boy was white-faced and grimacing, but there was no time to tend him now; all hands were needed. If the boy could no longer work, he could still serve the captain as a lookout on the quarterdeck.

"Tie him in; he'll not be able to keep footing on his own," the captain ordered Chippy as the big man let the boy down on the deck.

"Aye, sir." Chippy grimaced at the task. The boy was fairly bad off, with an arm out of place and his face ashen. "Are you fit for it?" Chippy leaned down to the boy.

"Lash me in." The boy's voice was strong, and I envied him his bravery. I turned my attention back to the main deck and watched the sailors as they pulled the huge sails, or tried to. Another boy, young Bobby Doyle, had taken Slattery's place on the ratlines and was up to cut the fore royal, the very top sail on the foremast.

A darker shade of black suddenly loomed over the ship; I glanced up expecting to see a cloud. I saw instead a wall of seawater over us, falling fast. All at once we were beneath it! The cold sea crashed on the deck, and I felt myself weightless, rolling sideways, tumbling with no hold, no air to cry out, even for my mother. The silence was overwhelming, a pitch-dark quiet. That was quickly replaced by the rush of air as the ship righted herself and

I was thrown, wet as a mop, on the opposite side of the quarterdeck and facing the other direction.

All around me were items that had no place on the deck: papers and maps from the captain's cabin, and a barrel of salt pork that had somehow made its way from below. As the ship evened out, the water on deck returned to the sea, sloshing over the sides. "Again!" I heard the captain holler, but I had no time to reason it out before I was plunged under once more, this time tossed against the sidewall of the captain's cabin, slammed hard enough to knock the air out of me. We stayed under, the ship taking on water as she lay on her side, the wave flowing out before sucking back in. I tried to gain some footing with my paws, but found only water below me as I pedaled.

Again the ship righted with a sick-making heave, and rolled over to her other side, sloshing between the waves. I slid down the side of the captain's cabin and landed on my feet in a puddle about as deep as I was tall. I shook myself, and a spray of water flew from my fur. It was then that I noticed that I could see my shadow cast on the deck before me. I assumed that could only mean one thing: the sun was breaking through the dark clouds. But when I looked up, the sky was not blue. It was a greenish yellow, like copper in need of a shine.

The ship rocked hard, back and forth, then evened out, with water pouring out of every hole and splashing down from the deck. I heard a thick slam as the door of the captain's cabin burst open, and a very dry and untouched first mate, Mr. Archer, came forth, kicking the wet sail and ropes that blocked his path. "You there, sailor!" he hollered at Chippy, making it all too apparent that he had not bothered to learn the sailors' names. "Can't you manage to keep this vessel steady? I'm positively ill from this heaving." He clasped his white hands over his belly and swayed with the ship, looking more green in the gills than ever.

Chippy leapt up to the quarterdeck and, in one swift motion, pulled Archer close to him. Holding Archer's head steady with his left hand, Chippy pulled back his thick right arm as if to bring his open palm across Archer's face. But he stopped himself, instead releasing the man, sending him sideways on the deck, scrambling to get away.

Archer sat up, stunned, and looked at Chippy's angry face looming over him. "What is the meaning—"

"You lily-livered fool, when we are in need of every hand aboard," Chippy barked. "I'm in no position to order you, as you are above me in station, but I will promise you this: if you've not found your way on deck to clear those sails in two clicks, you'll be on your back before this storm blows again." Chippy held up his fist and stood in a true fighter's stance, glaring at Archer with eyes cold as the sea herself.

Archer scrambled to his feet and leapt to the main deck, grabbing hold of a sail from one of the other sailors. He was hard at work in the grim yellow light that washed over the ship, helping the men before I could even catch my breath. I felt all hope go out of me—we were not yet through the storm. Could the *Melissa Rae* weather much more of this? Exhausted and damp to the end of my tail, I did not want to be grouped with the likes of Archer—scared and stupid to the ways of the sea. So I, too, leapt down to the main deck, and I tried to find my mother and what work we could do to help the men.

"Here's a sign," I heard from over my head as I was scooped up. "Look! We've still got our little rat!" Sean reported with a laugh. The sailors who were standing laughed weakly, and some sighed deep. From this height I could better see the damage on the main deck, and it was a sight to behold. The railing had been tossed from the gunwale all along one side, and one of the jolly boats was completely gone. The other jolly moved about unstowed, with so many boards missing, appearing too damaged to be of any use. The bigger longboat remained secured in the middle of the deck, but the hatch was thrown open wide, and I spied seawater inside. The remainder of the deck was no longer planks of brown wood, but instead was covered by yards and yards of wet white sail and rope. When Sean set me down on them, I was surprised to learn that the sails, which had looked so light and full of air when billowing above the ship, were really heavy, thick canvas, rough under the paws and now pounds heavier with rain and seawater.

Sean was barking out orders to the sailors standing: "All able men, move the injured sailors into quarters." Sean turned to the cook. "Moses, you'll go see to the captain and to Slattery." I watched as the man limped off, hopping on his good leg. "We'll need all who are left on deck to clear these sails. Have I two men who can begin the bailing from the central hatch?"

Not a word was spoken as the men went about their tasks. It was as if they were all in shock, the life ripped from their waterlogged bodies. I shook the water off me as best I could, and set about the ship in search of my mother. Crossing the deck was made easier by the sudden stillness of the sea, and harder by the slabs of wood and canvas sail that blocked my path.

"I'm in need of a sturdy man," I heard Moses call out from the quarterdeck. The tall blond fellow called Smyth quickly made his way up and around to the wheel. I stood stock-still. Could the captain be hurt? I had to know, so I turned and ran across the main deck, my wet tail tucked in behind me. The stairs to the quarterdeck had been washed away; I put out my claws and climbed the wet wood, making my way up to the captain's cabin.

There I saw Moses and Smyth untying the body of Slattery, who was still lashed where Chippy had roped him in. His head lolled strangely on his shoulders, and he reminded me, oddly enough, of a rag doll I had once seen Melissa holding. When Moses was done untying him, he put his hands on the young man's face for a moment, holding his eyes shut. He whispered something quietly and paused before moving the body with Smyth, whom I saw had watery eyes, as they walked past me. They carried him slowly, without urgency, and that was a sign to me: Slattery was not just injured anymore; there was nothing they could do to help him. Slattery's death was the first I had seen aboard, though, sadly, it would not be the last. Behind the men I caught sight of the captain. He was grimacing in pain, still tied fast to the wooden wheel, his eyes shut tight.

In a moment, Moses returned. Where he and Smyth had taken Slattery, I did not know. "Captain," he asked, "shall I tie off that leg for you? Might ease it a bit."

"You're needed more below." The captain bit back a cry of pain and opened his eyes. It was then that I noticed that his leg was turned around from his body, his foot almost pointing the wrong way.

"Ah, Captain. What good am I below? I'll get a bit of this wood we have floating around, and some rope, and we'll have you in shape before she blows again." With that Moses picked up a loose piece of the railing and a long lash of rope—the same rope that had held the young dead sailor in his place.

"My dear wife in heaven—ah, pray for me!" the captain cried out as Moses grasped his leg. In one quick motion he had righted the foot around to the front. "Oh God, the pain! Stop now, man! I beg you!"

"It will be a moment, sir; you've got to keep your wits. Here." Moses picked up another small slat of wood and set it in the captain's mouth. The captain bit down hard on the wood and clenched his eyes shut. I could barely stand to watch as Moses set the rail behind the captain's leg, wound the rope around it, and tightly tied it off. As he did, not a murmur escaped the captain's lips, though I felt sick in my belly at the pain he must be experiencing. "Better, sir?" Moses stared into the captain's white face. The captain nodded and spat the bit of wood out of his mouth.

The captain took a long deep breath. "I'll not forget this kindness, Mr. Moses," he said calmly, seeming to return to his old self. "Now back to deck and do what you can to keep this ship on the waves and not under them."

Moses nodded. "Aye, sir." He turned and was hobbling toward the main deck when he spied me. "Captain," Moses called out, motioning down at me before he moved on to join the other men.

The captain let out his whistle, the three-note one he used to call my mother, and I looked about, hoping to see her come. But she did not. "You there, cat!" the captain hollered. "Jacob Tibbs, come here." Then I realized: the whistle was for me. Terrified, I moved forward as fast as I could to where the captain stood on his one leg. His hands were white and rubbed raw where the wrists were tied to the wooden wheel, and I knew at once with great sadness that he would be unable to reach down and pick me up.

The captain coughed, and water came from his throat. "You're half your size soaking wet. How you've managed, I have no way of knowing." The captain's eyes drooped closed for a second; then he coughed hard and spit up more seawater. After a deep breath, he opened his eyes and looked right at me. "You're to find your mother and stay with her for the duration of this weather. Now go." With those words the captain slumped forward, his body leaning across the wheel, and he seemed to be a rag doll, too, held in place only by the ropes that bound him. I found my voice and mewed, a waterlogged gargle at first, then loud and clear, hoping someone would come to his aid, for surely he would die tied here to the wheel. But the sky was slowly growing dark, and the waves were once again pounding the ship, my cries drowned beneath the noise.

And here is where I had to make my choice: to leave the captain and find my mother, as I had been ordered, or stay with the man who made this ship my home, protecting him as I could. I knew the captain had been lashed to the wheel so that he could steer the *Melissa Rae* through the storm. Now his limp body hung on the spokes as the ship made a hard starboard turn. Perhaps I could wake him? I had little time to consider my options as a huge wall of water—twice as tall as the *Melissa Rae*—suddenly struck the ship, and I found myself trapped between the captain's good leg and the base of the wooden wheel, under the dark, cold water, my eyes again stinging in the brine.

The ship righted herself and pitched to the other side as I latched onto the captain's leg. I knew not what to do—surely, this was the end. With no captain to steer the ship, we were all lost, to a one. Without a moment more of deliberation, I dug my claws into his leg and sent my teeth in as well. I prayed not to hurt him, but only to wake him from his unconscious state. And I was successful! As the water slopped off the deck, the captain jerked his leg in pain and coughed awake. I looked up to see him grasp the wheel and turn us in the right direction, away from the storm, just as another black wave closed over our heads.

CHAPTER 8

NINE LIVES

When I came to, all was dark and still. I could see nothing, even with my night eyes, and quickly realized I was still tucked up inside the captain's trouser leg. I shimmied out and plopped onto the waterlogged deck. I first noticed the stars overheard. Bright, sharp, and lovely, they shone down from a freshly washed sky, drifting behind puffy bits of clouds.

The captain was still tied to and slumped over the huge wheel. But I could not see any sign of misfortune, no blood or pale skin. I scratched at his ankle, just lightly, and he twitched a bit, as if in a dream, but it was enough to tell me he was still living. A lantern came our way, and I recognized the blond sailor called John Smyth carrying it.

Smyth whistled through his piano-key teeth. "Will ya 'ave a look at that! The little wee kitty—" Just then, Smyth caught sight of the captain slumped over the wheel. "Cap, are you shtill with us?" He touched the captain's shoulder and shook him gently. The captain rattled awake and coughed up a bit of water.

Smyth put the lantern near his face. "You all there, Cap?" he asked, and the captain gave a nod, turning his head to the side to cough out more liquid.

"I'll undo your ties now." Smyth put the lantern on the deck and began unknotting the ropes that held the captain to the wheel.

"Mind the leg, man, and steady as you go," the captain said, his voice a rasp, and Smyth glanced down. I looked, too, and saw that the captain's bad leg was swollen up to twice the size of his good one; the ropes that Moses had used to secure it now cut deep into the flesh. He held his foot at an unnatural angle, and I knew something was terribly wrong.

"We'll have Moses take a look-shee at that, Cap, and you'll be good as new," Smyth said nervously. I could tell he was as worried as I was about the captain.

When the ropes were undone, Smyth helped the captain over to his cabin and took him within. I followed behind them as close as the door and then leapt down to the main deck to survey the damage.

The second half of the storm had done little more than the first, as the sailors had had a bit of time to batten down in the middle of it. Now the men walked around on deck, each holding a lantern, doing what they could in the dark to make repairs. Most important seemed the pumping and the bailing. The *Melissa Rae* was sitting heavy at sea, the bilge full to brimming with ocean and rainwater.

The sailors said there was no chance of making speed again until she was bailed entirely.

I watched the fellows pitch and pump, calling out to one another in the dark, and walked the deck to find my mother. When I went below deck to check the galley, I heard moans coming from the sailors' quarters, so I poked my nose in to investigate. I'd not been in this part of the ship before, but I knew by its smell that this was where the sailors must spend most of their time. Each man had a hammock here, and the odor of chewing tobacco, smoke, seawater, and sweat was overwhelming. Rocking in his hammock in the pitch black was Dougherty, the big fellow with the black muttonchop whiskers. The other sailors admired Dougherty as the strongest man aboard; a former fighter, he, along with Chippy, would do most of the heavy lifting required on our trip. But now his arm was set in a canvas sling cut from a downed sail, and he was cradling it. I jumped up to his hammock to see what the trouble was.

"Ugh." Dougherty tried to kick me off. "Vermin!" I meowed to let him know that it wasn't a rat come to visit him; it was just I, Jacob Tibbs.

I meowed again, and Dougherty whispered, "Is that you, Mrs. Tibbs? Your ghost haunting me already?" I meowed again, confused, thinking the man delirious in his pain, and crawled up to rest beside his barrel-sized chest.

He sighed, relieved. "So it's Mrs. Tibbs's little one, looking for a bit of comfort?" Dougherty asked. "Aye, mate, come on up here, as I know just how you feel. I lost me mum when I was but a wee lad meself." Dougherty gently rocked the hammock and whispered, "Ah, the pain of this shoulder is terrible, but I feel for you, young Tibbs. And I'm sorry for your loss." Then the big man sang a bit, quietly, an old sea song about missing one's mum, and soon I could hear him breathing deeply, his snores rattling through the hammock. Once I knew he was well asleep, I leapt down and crept out of the sailors' quarters, still puzzling over his words. Yes, I had lost sight of my mother during the worst of the storm, but I was on my way to find her, and this ship was only so big. I was sure my mother was looking for me, too, and that we would not be apart for long.

Back on the deck, I could see a sliver of light on the horizon behind us. The sun was rising just as it had yesterday over the ship, but this time there was no pink in the sky as it came up. A clear sky in the morning was meant to be a good sign, that's what the sailors said. I moved to the front of the ship and stood as I had yesterday with my mother, right at the cathead by the anchor, staring out over the sea as the pale, watery gray light of dawn washed across the deck. I noticed that the feeling of fear from yesterday was gone. It was good to have that rock no longer in my belly.

As a matter of fact, there was nothing in my belly, nor could I remember the last time I had nursed, and the rumbling sent me again in search of my mother. I crossed the deck to the starboard side and tried to stay out of the way of the sailors as they repaired the railing in the dim light.

"How do you like that?" I heard Chippy say from over my head. "We've lost Slattery, and that little rat made it through. I never would've thought it so."

"Aye," murmured Sean, stroking his beard, "but more's the pity. I don't believe he's weaned, so he'll no doubt follow Mrs. Tibbs down. A shame."

"Pity not, he'd be no good to us. No place for him on board." Chippy turned back to his work as if I weren't even there.

An urgency went through me then. Why were the sailors all speaking this way about my mother? Had she been hurt? The image of Slattery flashed into my mind, his head lolling around on his neck. Where was my mother? I had to find out, and meowed up to Sean to get his attention. He continued his work as well, so I mewed again, long and high. Finally he sighed and dropped the tools he was holding, turning to look down at me.

While Chippy glared, Sean picked me up and carried me gently to the central hatch. "There you are, mate. Say your good-byes for now; we'll send them off as soon as the sun is up." Sean plunked me down on the deck beside the body of the young sailor, Slattery. He was stretched out on his back and looked as though he were sleeping. He'd been wrapped in his hammock with just his face showing. His eyes were shut, his lips pale, and his cheek was cold where I touched it with my nose.

Beside him, tucked in our basket, was my mother, also sleeping. She was curled in and under the stuffing, looking warm and snug. Relief washed over me: I had found

Mother! I leapt into our basket to surprise her, but she did not stir. When I nudged her side and tried to rouse her, I found that she, too, was cold. Why would she not wake?

I felt a hand on my back then, and looked to see Bobby Doyle kneeling beside me, his yellow hair dark and wet, just combed and braided. "When the lines broke last night, down they both came, man and cat. She tumbled so, I thought, 'She's landed feetfirst, and she's with us'—but it wasn't to be. Slattery, poor lad, held on for a bit, but . . ." He didn't finish his thought.

It took a moment for me to understand his words. My mother would not wake, not ever? I thought of how Moses had held his hand over Slattery's face and closed his eyes, whispering something to the boy though he was already gone. I licked Mother's face and smoothed her white whiskers back, the way she liked them. Tired and hungry, I longed to curl up beside her, the way I always did, but I knew somehow it wouldn't be right. Where she was to go now, I did not know. But I could not go with her. I longed for our days below deck with my brothers and sisters. When Mother was near, I would always be safe. As I stood beside our basket, the sun rose over the ship. It was but my second day at sea, and I was entirely alone.

CHAPTER 9

SHIP'S CAT

The sun rose, and light washed across the deck. Still I stood at my mother's basket, not knowing what else to do in my sorrow. A hand closed around my middle as the bells rang six o'clock in the morning. "Come on, little fellow. I know shomeone who'd like a word with you." Smyth picked me up and carried me across the deck and toward the captain's cabin. "I've just told the cap about your mum, and he's taken it hard. But sheeing you might cheer him. Put on a brave face, mate," he added, looking down at me as he knocked on the captain's door.

"'Tis Smyth, shir, with a visitor."

"Enter," the captain called from within.

"Master Jacob Tibbs, is it?" the captain said as he saw me. The great man was stretched out on his bed, his clothes and hair rumpled. His trouser leg had been cut away up to the thigh, and his lower leg was secured with a wooden plank, held in place by thick strips of fabric. He motioned to a chair beside him, then spoke to the sailor. "Mr. Smyth, send in Mr. Archer and Mr. Reid before the next bell. That will be all."

Smyth plopped me into the chair, then closed the door behind him, and the captain's blue eyes were upon me entirely. I realized that I had never been in the presence of the man alone, and I felt myself shake with fear. I wasn't fit to be sitting in this fancy velvet chair, and certainly not to take the captain's attention. What would my mother have thought of this?

"Master Jacob Tibbs," the captain said sadly, "you've come to keep me company here, have you? We can share our sadness." He sighed. "I did not listen to your mother, Jacob, and now pay the price, not only with her life but with that of a young Christian sailor, Mr. Slattery. I take the responsibility for both lives, for your loss."

The captain paused and grimaced in pain, clutching the top part of his thigh. He let out a heavy sigh and turned to me again.

"Many a sailor thought me insane to prattle on as I did to your mother," he continued. A quick knock at the door interrupted the rest of his statement.

"'Tis Smyth, with Archer and Reid, shir," a voice came from outside.

"Enter," the captain called out, and the two men ducked into the cabin.

Archer walked in and looked around the room. "I could've sworn I heard you talking to someone, Captain," he said. Then, shaking his head, he made to sit in the chair where I was perched and very nearly crushed the life out of me. When he noticed I was beneath him, he leapt up and tried to shoo me from my seat. "Scat, you flea-bitten vermin," he hissed. "How many of these creatures are on this ship? They are constantly underfoot."

The captain glared and cleared his throat. "If I desire your extended presence in my cabin, Mr. Archer, I will ask you to seat yourself. As it is, I do not. You will stand for your orders. And before you say another unkind word about my new ship's cat, I beg your attention here." With much effort, the captain pulled up his cuff around his good leg, and I saw two red claw marks and, between, an angry, swollen-looking bite—my marks from the day before. As I peered closer, I could see small red dots where each one of my teeth had sunk into the captain's leg. I certainly hadn't intended to attack him so furiously, and I was horrified by what I had done. I looked to the captain's eyes but found no anger there. Was he not terribly displeased with me?

"I was unconscious, tied to the wheel, and something sharp—some pins sticking into my leg—woke me. It was enough for me to gain my wits and steer this ship to safety. I am sure you can each recognize that those marks were made by young Master Jacob here, so indeed you have him to thank for the very fact that you are alive today. He saved our ship and every one of us."

If a cat can smile, I was smiling then, and I sat firmly on my velvet cushion, enjoying the tongue-lashing that Archer took standing up. Sean Reid stood beside him, seeming to enjoy it as well.

With that the captain pushed his cuff down and demanded, "Men, report on the ship's condition."

Sean began. "Captain, the tween deck is all but bailed out. The rail of the starboard side is off, but we've rigged a rope and what remains of the wood in the place of it, for now. We can likely use wood from the damaged jolly boat to finish it. As it is, no one will fall over, save maybe Master Jacob, if he's not careful." Sean glanced at me and gave a little wink. "The hold is dry as a bone. And we 'ave one sailor down, sir: Dougherty, with his shoulder out again. Moses says he can have that right in a day's time." Sean lowered his head and stepped back.

"And what of your report, Mr. Archer?" The captain turned to his reluctant first mate and waited for a reply.

"Ah, all is just as Sean reported," Archer stumbled. I wondered if he would include the details of how Chippy had held him by his collar and almost put him on his back. But he did not tattle. Instead he stood mute before the captain.

"Do we not have two dead to cast overboard?" the captain asked.

"We've only one dead, sir, a young sailor," Archer said. After an awkward pause, he finally cleared his throat and added, "Oh, and the cat, of course." The callous way in which he spoke of my mother made my claws come out.

"And do you wish to do the honors, Mr. Archer, or shall I?" the captain asked.

"Honors, sir? Wha . . . oh, yes the honors, indeed." Archer swallowed hard. "Ah, you shall—I mean to say that you will have the honors, sir, as this is your ship," he said.

"And as you've no bloody idea what you're doing," Sean cut in with a harsh whisper.

"Enough!" barked the captain. "Mr. Reid, I'm surprised at you. Do you not know better than to address the first officer that way?"

"Sir, if I may, it is Mr. Archer's responsibility that we've lost Slattery and Mrs. Tibbs. If only he'd listened to reason—"

The captain cut him off. "I'll not have blame cast upon any but myself. It was my own decision to put up full sails yesterday, and my own decision to sail through. So you'll kindly hold your tongue on the issue."

The captain looked at both of the men standing before him. "I'll need to be carried out to the main deck. In Mr. Dougherty's absence, send back Mr. MacNeil for the job. Mr. Archer, you'll ring for all hands for the proceedings. Let's have this done with haste, as I've not the heart for it. Dismissed."

With that the men filed out of the cabin, and I alone held the captain's attention. As I leapt down from my chair, I paused by his side, and he reached down and gently petted my back for a moment. I nudged his hand with my head, longing for a scratch behind the ears. "Go on then, Jacob," he sighed. "You've work to do, my lad." I saw a small, sad smile cross his face as I went out through the door that the men had left ajar.

The bell rang for all hands, and the sailors gathered at the starboard bulwark of the ship. They stood without speaking, in a semicircle around the body of young Slattery and the basket where my mother lay. Slattery's face was now covered; he had been sewn up into his hammock completely. Mother was in her basket, curled up as if asleep, the calico cloth that Melissa had given us just days before we left port now tucked in around her. She looked peaceful, her whiskers just as she liked them to be, her fur orderly. I longed to see her wake, to feel her loving gaze on me, one last time.

Sean carried a sturdy chair down to the deck for the captain to sit in, as Chippy supported the captain's weight and helped him make his way down on his one good leg.

"I'll not need that," Captain Natick said, waving away Sean and the chair that he offered. "These two honorable sailors deserve a proper burial, and a captain who can stand and deliver the last words before they are committed to the deep." The captain leaned against the railing and grimaced in pain as Chippy took his arm from around his shoulder, yet he stood on his own weight. Clearly, the pain was overwhelming, the bleak task at hand making the situation all the worse.

"Please bow your heads," the captain said, his voice strong and clear despite the fact that his face was blanched white, his brow wet with perspiration.

I stood fast beside my mother's basket and looked

down at my white front paws. I was overwhelmed with a sudden grief: my mother had loved me despite all my shortcomings—my small size, my four mittens, my wobbly sea legs—but would anyone else in my life ever be so forgiving? Melissa had been right—that was what it was to have a mother, and now mine was gone.

"John Slattery, aged nineteen years. This was his third journey across the Atlantic, the second aboard the *Melissa Rae.* He was an honorable sailor, and is survived by his wife and infant son, who shares his name. We commit his body to the sea, in God's name, and his soul to heaven. Amen."

"Amen," the sailors all murmured in response. Then Chippy and Sean each took up a side of the hammock and gently lifted it to the railing. The captain made the sign of the cross over the body just as the two sailors released it over the side. A second of silence, then a splash.

"Mrs. Tibbs, a captain's cat who knows no equal. She sailed countless journeys with me aboard the *Melissa Rae.* She is survived by the many litters of healthy kittens she bore in her lifetime, and by Master Jacob Tibbs." The captain paused to look at me, and I saw tears well in his eyes, almost spilling down his pale cheeks. His voice broke as he continued, "We commit her body to the sea, in God's name, and her soul to heaven. Amen."

I heard Sean sniffle as he leaned down to grasp my mother's basket by one handle; Chippy's eyes were bloodshot but his face a stone, his jaw clenched as he reached down for the other handle. I realized all at once what they meant to do—to throw my mother into the sea, as they had done with Slattery! Was I never to see my mother again? Without a second thought I leapt up into the basket as they lifted it, and I nestled against my mother's body—now gone very cold and unyielding. I breathed in her scent and shut my eyes, trying to block out the sailors, the sea, and the hard knowledge that she was truly gone.

"Now, kitten," Sean said, still sniffling, "you're to stay here with us. Where your Mrs. Tibbs goes now, you cannot follow." He tried to lift me gently from the basket with one hand, but I held fast to the cloth with my claws, scrabbling to cling to my spot, and the calico that had been around my mother came up with me. Sean placed me back on the deck, the cloth still under my paws.

The two sailors carried the basket to the railing, where Captain Natick made the sign of the cross over her. "Godspeed, my truest friend," the captain whispered. In an instant the basket disappeared over the side of the ship, and a splash was heard. I paced the deck where the basket had been, circling, smelling the wood for a scent of my mother. Then I meowed and kneaded the cloth with my paws in agony. I knew not what to do now, so I crouched where her basket had been, just moments before, and I cried a mournful mewing. I curled into a tight ball, barely aware of the sailors around me as they quietly dispersed and went back to their jobs.

"Let him alone," the captain ordered when Chippy went to move me out of the way. "He'll come around; he's a Tibbs, after all." I heard the captain shuffle back to his cabin with Chippy's help. As Sean leaned down to move the chair, he ran his hand over my small back and whispered to me, "There, there, little one. There, there."

And then I was alone. The sailors were all occupied on the damaged ship, some getting their first sleep in many hours, others tackling the much-needed repairs. I lay on the cloth in a tight ball, feeling sorry for myself in my hunger and sadness until I drifted off to sleep, lulled by the sound and the rocking of the ocean, knowing that my mother was now part of this huge body of water that we floated upon, though I would never lay eyes on her again.

CHAPTER 10

THE KITCHEN RAT

When I woke, all was dark. I stood and quickly knocked my head on something hard—and hot! I yelped and lay on my belly—I was trapped!

"You're awake, then, are you?" I heard Moses, the ship's cook, call to me.

As my eyes adjusted to the murky scene I saw Moses's face looming large and close to mine; a golden loop that I'd not noticed before dangled from one of his earlobes. "Come on, then, let's try a bit of grub."

He reached toward me with one tattooed hand and grabbed my front paws, dragging me out into the galley. I had been tucked in under the stout stove that he used for cooking. "You've slept for almost two days, Master Jacob. Thought we'd lost you as well." Moses plopped me down on the galley's wooden sideboard and petted my back. "You look a sight, you do," he laughed. "And I'll barter that you're in need of this." Moses slid a thick wooden bowl under my nose and leaned back on the counter to watch me. "Well, have a go, then," he urged. I looked down into the bowl and saw another cat staring up at me. I leapt back with a cry. Was it one of my brothers, also on board the ship? Perhaps I wasn't alone after all.

"My lands!" Moses laughed. "That's just you, Jacob; that's your reflection there in the broth," he said, pushing the bowl close to my front paws again. I gazed in and saw a tiny cat face looking up at me—my own—my fur and whiskers all askew from my sleep under the stove. I knew at once what my mother would think of my appearance, and she would not be pleased.

Before I could set to cleaning myself, my head was pushed down, my nose and mouth deep in the bowl of liquid. I came up, gasping for air and shaking my face. "That's how it's done, lad. Have a taste," Moses urged. He had always seemed so kind; I had no idea why now he had suddenly taken a harsh turn—pushing my head into the broth.

I licked my nose clean and tried to back away from the bowl, but Moses held me firm and again pushed my head into the broth. "Just have a bit of it, kitty, come on, then," he urged. I struggled and made to lick my face clean. The taste of the broth was salty . . . and good. My stomach lurched in hunger. This time I stepped to the bowl and put my own face down, trying to get a bit more into my mouth. At first I wanted to put my mouth into the bowl and drink it like I had done with my mother's milk, but I soon got the idea that my tongue would bring the delicious fish broth to my mouth for me, and that my nose didn't even need to touch the surface. When the soup was gone, I licked the bottom of the wooden bowl with my tongue, collecting every last drop. It was then that I noticed I had an audience, a few sailors who had come into the galley.

"Care for a bit more?" Sean asked. He ladled another slop of soup into the bowl, and I dunked my face low, to lap it up as fast as I could.

"Not so fast, lad, you'll make yourself sick," Moses said.

But Sean was elated. "A good omen, that," he said, slapping Moses on the back.

When I finished the second bowl of soup, I mewed for still more. "Your belly's dragging the floor, mate!" Moses laughed and poked my very rounded midsection. "Let's see how that sits before you have extra servings." He put me down on the floor beside the warm stove. I could see that Moses had tucked my bit of the calico from Mother's basket behind the stove, and I dragged myself there now, curling up on the cloth, listening as the other sailors from the forenoon watch came into the galley for their grub.

"The runt's well, then, is he?" I heard Chippy growl, after being told of my soup-eating success. He shoved a piece of hardtack biscuit into his mouth after using it to sop up the rest of his own bowl of soup. "So be it, but if you've a mind to share any of our grub with that cat, think again," he cautioned Moses. "Mrs. Tibbs made her diet of rats and vermin, not fish soup. Sooner that runt learns his place on this ship, the better." He pushed his chair back and left the galley, grabbing another of the flat biscuits on his way out the door.

"Chippy's right, sadly," Sean admitted. "We've barely enough grub on board to keep ourselves for this trip, not a bit to spare."

"That's the doing of Archer's Shipping—tightest-fisted company I've ever sailed under." Moses nodded. "One extra bag of flour and he threatened to have me put off the ship—told me I'd not find work on the Liverpool docks again anytime soon, as well. He's a strict runner, that one."

"I don't fancy this soup much myself," one of the younger sailors said. "The wee cat can have what's left." He pushed his wooden bowl to the middle of the table.

"And mine as well," Dougherty said, also pushing in his bowl. I noticed that his arm was still held fast to his chest in a tight white sling, but from his face he looked his old self again.

"We'll make do until Jacob can fend for himself," Sean agreed. "And if Archer's none the wiser, no harm done."

"Aye," the young sailor agreed. "That cat makes the captain happy, and it's good luck to have him aboard. He can share my grub until he's fit."

Dougherty nodded. "We've all got our jobs to do. Jacob will learn his in time."

The sailors' words washed over me as my limbs grew heavy. I longed to purr in Dougherty's ear, to let him know how I appreciated his kindness, but my eyes closed, my head nodded, and I was asleep before the sailors were done with their conversation.

Later I woke to laughing and a great banging and sloshing sound. Moses was serving first dogwatch their grub and washing up the pots and pans in seawater and lye soap. Hours and hours had passed, and as I peered out from under the stove, I could see that the lanterns were now lit.

"How'd you get her hands off you, lad?" I heard Moses ask.

"I says to the miss, 'You'll have a new one, luv, but not off me!' " A dark-haired sailor laughed as he told his story.

"You'll not visit that port again!" Chippy's deep voice boomed through the small galley. "Now, 'ave I told you all of the time I found myself in Wales?" he asked, leaning back in his chair and putting his boots on the table.

Suddenly Moses stomped hard with his peg leg, interrupting Chippy's tale and scaring a little dark shadow off a bag of flour. "Go, you! Scat!" Moses waved his arms. "These vermin, it's as if they've a mind to the fact that Mrs. Tibbs has left us. A bite of food out and they're up on the sideboard and climbing over me face in my sleep."

The sailors went quiet for a moment, and I wondered why. "On with your story, then, Chippy," Moses said, looking back to the men at the table. He seemed to know all at once that he'd said too much—especially with Chippy in earshot.

Chippy put his chair legs on the floor with a loud thud

and stood. "Where is he? Where's that wee kitty you're keeping, Moses?" I scooted back under the stove, hiding myself as best I could, but it was no use. Chippy reached beneath the stove and caught me. Fast as lightning, he grabbed me by my middle and plunked me on the bag of flour. "Earn your keep, runt. There's rats all through this ship, and I, for one, have grown weary of being woken by a vermin bite in my hammock." Chippy stood looming over me, waiting for what, I did not know. I looked to Moses, but he wouldn't meet my eyes—just busied himself with the washing. The room was quiet except for the sound of Moses's soggy rag, sloshing over the pots.

Chippy moved to the sideboard and caught up a large knife by its handle. He stood and looked at me with such venom, my breathing all but stopped.

"It's not as bad as all that—come now, Chip, have some brandy." Moses stepped between Chippy and myself, putting his hands up to protect me, but he was a much smaller man, and I knew that if Chippy had a mind to do me harm, no one in the room would be able to stop him.

Chippy pushed Moses aside and brought the knife down hard on the counter—slicing a bite of cheese from the block that was sitting there. "I've no mind to hurt your little pet," Chippy said, his voice sounding a bit sore, as if the mere insinuation had insulted him. "But I will teach him a lesson."

He took the piece of cheese and placed it beside me on the bag of flour. "Here, rat, here's your grub—come and at it," he called out. The room was quiet again as everyone watched and waited.

"D'ya remember how Misshus Tibbs would leave a line of ratsh outshide the cap'sh door in the morning?" Smyth said. "She was a hunter, that one, and always made the man shmile, she did." He shook his head and took a long swig from a brown bottle the sailors were passing around. "It'd be a pleasure to shee the cap happy like that again."

"She had seven there one dawn, didn't she?" Dougherty asked the others. "Seven rats, lined up and bloodied. I think we didn't see another whisker of vermin for the rest of that trip out." The sailors laughed at the happy memory, but I felt sad. Though warmed by their kind words about my mother, picturing her in the heroic way they described made me miss her all the more. But the moment did not last long. Suddenly I was aware that I was no longer alone atop the bag: a dark, furry creature had joined me.

This was not a fellow cat. He was almost as big as I was, but his face was different. He had whiskers, but they were small and bent. He was dirty, his fur a matted gray, and his eyes! Oh, the eyes of a rat are a terrible thing the first time you behold them! Small and yellow, his eyes told me all that he was in an instant—a terrible creature, a sworn enemy. Worse yet were his teeth: big and sharp, they stood out from his mouth even when it was closed. And when he opened his jaws at me and hissed . . . ! I jumped down from the bag and ran, quick as I could, back to my calico cloth behind the stove. From there I watched

as the creature pounced upon the cheese and, with one more hiss in my direction, disappeared down behind the bags of flour.

"That rat's about as big as our ship's cat!" Bobby Doyle laughed.

"It's not a matter for laughing," Chippy cut in, and all the sailors went quiet. "Moses, you'll not give that cat any more fish-head soup, or anything to eat, for that matter. You'll make him soft—why should he work for his meals if he knows he can always find something from you?"

Moses kept his eyes on his scrubbing and mumbled a reply that I couldn't hear.

"We all work aboard the *Melissa Rae* to earn our keep," Chippy went on, "and this cat will earn his grub, too, or he'll be put overboard." With that he picked up his hat and stormed out of the galley. Even the rattle of the floorboards under his boots was terrifying to me—he was right: I was nothing more than a coward, and a freeloader at that.

"What do you s'pose has gotten him so off about poor Jacob?" Doyle asked the others. "Jacob's but a baby cat."

Smyth shrugged. "He's more off about Archer, but he can't rightly hit 'im in the gob, now can 'e?"

"'Tis easier to blame a wee kitty for all our problems aboard," Moses agreed, looking up from his scrub work, "but he almost scared the little lad from his wits there!"

The other sailors gathered up their things and thanked Moses for the meal as they left the galley. But even after they were gone, the tension remained thick and silent.

When it was just Moses and myself, Moses stopped his scrubbing for a moment and came to pet my back. "Jacob, the boys are right. Chippy is angry, but not at you, lad. You take your time and get well; then we'll learn you how to catch a rat or two. Sleep now, and there will be more broth for you when you wake."

CHAPTER 11

THE WAR BEGINS

I took Moses's words to heart and did rest as much as I could. Though the sailors usually slept only a few hours at a time, I found that I could sleep soundly in my spot behind the stove for hours on end, especially when Chippy was not to be found in the galley. Sometimes the men would call me out and bring me a bit of string for play when they were in for meals. Sean tied a knot on the end of untwined rope and attached it to a stool leg so I had something to bat at. It was my only toy, and as I was still a kitten, I could play with that ball of frayed rope for ages until I grew tired and napped again. Unlike the sailors, I was not ever called to the deck in the middle of my sleep, and so the days passed in a uniform fashion for me: drinking up fish-head soup until I was fat and sleepy, visiting with the still-wounded captain in his quarters, and making my way around the ship, learning its every nook and cranny, but all the while wary of the vermin that shared this space with me. Occasionally I would see a flash of gray, a shadow of a long, thin tail, and I would turn and run straight back to my hiding spot beneath the stove.

When the bells rang out for afternoon watch, I would wait outside the captain's quarters. This was when Moses would bring the captain his midday meal, and I could scoot in the open door and visit for a while. Afternoon watch was usually when the captain was at his best, too. For as the night came on and the bell rang for first watch, I would find him sleeping and feverish, in a fretful slumber that would last until the dawn broke. The captain was so delirious at times that he would confuse me for my mother. "Ah, Mrs. Tibbs, come sit with me," he would say, petting my head and scratching me roughly behind the ears, the way he had done with my mother. It made me sad to see the captain in such poor health, as he had always appeared so strong; now he was forgetful and constantly fraught with the pain that his broken and infected limb had brought on.

Moses, the only sailor on board with any doctoring skills, attended to him as best he could, but still I would hear the sailors in the galley talk of horrible, impossible things.

"And the good captain today, is he well?" Sean asked.

"His fever comes on every night," Moses said. "And the wound on his leg smells foul; even cleaning it with brine makes no difference."

"If to cut it off saves the man, what's the wait?" Archer asked one night. "Chippy has a saw in his tools—let's be done with it!"

I saw a few of the men shift uncomfortably at Archer's harsh words. He was first mate, and in the captain's absence he was to be the chief officer of the ship. But the sailors had little respect for him, and his bluster often went ignored. On this night, Moses responded.

"As one who has been through the pain of a limb off," he said, "I hope we can keep the captain from it. It's no life for a man such as him."

"You've made out all right, Moses," Chippy said. "In fact, with your trousers, I rightly forget that you've only one leg!" He laughed and turned to the other men in the room. "Is there another sailor aboard who can turn a jig as well?"

"How was it that you lost it, man?" Archer asked Moses, and the galley fell quiet. I noticed that the other sailors were suddenly very busy eating their grub and looking down at their hands. There was an awkward stillness before Moses finally spoke again.

"I did not lose it; it was taken from me," Moses said, trying for a laugh that didn't come. When it was clear that Archer was still waiting for an answer, Moses grabbed up a kitchen cloth, dried his hands, and reached into the cabinet for a bottle of brown drink. "It's time for the captain's nip of this," he said, making his way to the door. "Helps to keep the pain at bay, and the fever as well. Chippy, when you've done, take that pot from the stove?" Usually

I would follow close behind Moses, hoping for a visit with the captain, but I knew that if I went this night, I would miss an interesting exchange, so I jumped up on Sean's lap for a scratch behind the ears and to listen.

After Moses was out of earshot, Archer looked around at the relieved faces of the sailors. "Obviously, I've asked something he hasn't an answer for, is that it?"

"He's an answer; it's just long in the telling." Sean spoke quietly and met Archer's eyes. "If you'd seen the man's back, you'd know better what he's been through. His hide is cross-marked with raised scars from so many beatings, I wonder if he can number them."

I licked my front paw and scrubbed my face clean as I listened to the sailors. I myself had seen Moses in his sleeping shirt, but had never taken notice of his back. Surely it couldn't be as bad as Archer's—the pink and splotchy color it took on when he removed his shirt on deck. Or Smyth's, which was peeling and had ugly brown spots all over it.

"I've heard that when he was a boy, he was made to work on a slaver with a horribly cruel captain. He never speaks of it," Dougherty added, scraping his soup bowl with a piece of hardtack.

"Is this true?" Archer said, suddenly more curious. "He was indentured? It's a wonder he gave up that line of work. He could have made an excellent profit."

"Running slaves is criminal, and he's not the stomach to see men and women sold like meat, beaten and locked up," Chippy growled. "Have you?" On nights when

Chippy had been drinking from the brown bottle and got gruff, I usually hid myself behind the stove to keep out of his way. But tonight I stayed on Sean's lap to hear what Archer might have to say for himself.

"Not I," Archer responded quickly. "But there are some who still run slavers, and they make a great deal of money." Archer looked somewhat nervous. "In fact, they turn a profit of two or three times the *Melissa Rae*."

Sean put his hand under me and scooped me from his lap before standing to put his wooden bowl into Moses's washbasin. "Slaving's a bad, dirty business, no matter what coin it brings"—and he locked eyes once more with Archer, who suddenly looked away.

As Sean opened the door to the galley, I slid out with him, wove my way around his feet, and quickly made up to the deck, where now the stars were full out and the *Melissa Rae* moved swift and silent through the still night sea. It had not been wise to stay below and listen in on the gossip and arguments. The sailors' talk had left me feeling sad and a bit lost. I knew now that Moses, who had been the most kind to me, had been treated very badly in his life, and that was a knowledge I did not want to have. Their talk about the captain also made me especially worried for his health, and I longed to see him.

Outside the captain's quarters, I could see a sliver of light beneath the door; Moses was still inside. I went to lift my paw and scratch at the door when I heard, from within, a quiet singing—Moses's voice in a tune. I did not know the words, but still the song was lovely, and I knew

Moses was trying to soothe the captain's pain, as he did on some nights when the fever was terribly bad.

> *It is of a flash packet,*
> *A packet of fame.*
> *She is bound to New York;*
> *The* Melissa Rae*'s her name.*
> *She is bound to the west'ard*
> *Where the stormy winds blow.*
> *Bound away to the west'ard,*
> *Good Lord, let her go.*

I lay outside the wooden door and listened to his voice, and the slap of the waves against the ship, and I wished and hoped with my entire small being that the captain would find his health again. I could not bear the thought of him being sewn into a hammock, like Slattery was, and thrown over the side of the ship. Whenever I thought of Slattery, the image of my mother, curled in our basket, came into my mind as well, though I tried never to think of that day. She had looked only asleep, but that was not so—she was never to wake. I preferred to remember her as she had been: brave, agile, and strong, but also warm and loving.

I wondered after what the sailors had said, some nights ago, about my mother's hunting skills and how she would leave a line of dead vermin outside the captain's door. If I could do the same, if I could capture one of the rats that plagued the ship and ate into the sailor's food, spreading their fleas and dirt where they pleased, perhaps I could also bring a smile to the captain's face. Suddenly I leapt to my paws—I knew at once what I needed to do to help the captain mend! It would not be easy, as the rats had had the run of the ship since my mother's passing, and they had grown fat and bold.

I looked at the open hatch to the tween deck and took in a deep breath of fresh night air before making my way stealthily down the ladder into the dark. I came to a second hatch that would lead me down into the hold, and it was closed tight. I tried it with my paws, but to no avail. I knew of another hatch, amidships, that was sometimes kept open to air the stores below. I crossed the tween deck in the dark and found it open. I descended into the hold, where I had never ventured alone before, placing one paw carefully in front of the other. As my eyes adjusted to the dark and the parcels took shape around me in the murky black, I perked my ears, put my tail into the air, and made myself a promise: I would not come up until I had a rat to place outside the captain's door, no matter how long it took.

CHAPTER 12

THE KILL

Below the deck was not a totally foreign place to me; I had lived down in the galley with my mother and siblings for some weeks following my birth. In fact, until my mother brought me topside on the day we left port, below deck was my whole world. But I had not set paw in the hold since my mother's passing—and since I had learned that the terrible rats I so feared kept themselves hidden there as well.

Straight below the main deck, or what the sailors called between decks, was where the galley and the sailors' sleeping quarters were located. But underneath that was the wide-open space that made up the whole basement of the ship, which we called the hold. Now as I made my way across the barrels and crates, the place took on a new meaning to me. Mother had brought me here once or twice, just the two of us, after my siblings had all been taken away by other captains. I was still so small then, she had carried me down into the hold, and roamed the length of it. I realized only now what she must have been doing: searching for her hated foes, the rats, before the *Melissa Rae* was loaded for the next journey.

When I had been below with my mother, there had been no parcels here. The *Melissa Rae* had been unloaded before Mother gave birth to us, so we found ourselves in a long, open space, the length of the entire ship, with only posts lining the middle to support the weight of the decks, and the bases of the three masts, as big around as tree trunks. On either side of the hold were metal bars that spanned from top to bottom, forming caged sections used to store the heaviest goods and keep them in their spots, so as to even out the balance of the ship.

Here was where the real employment of the *Melissa Rae* happened, yet no sailor ever had to work in the hold, nor set foot there, for the whole journey! This was the place that held all the goods that the captain and crew would sell or deliver once we reached land: the sixty huge rolls of cotton cloth, newly woven, thirty more of cloth with fine small stripes, and one hundred of chintz, a patterned fabric. The rolls were long—each of them took up at least twenty feet across the bottom of the hold—and were either wrapped around a wooden pole or rolled so that a hollow tunnel ran through the entire length—a tunnel that was just big enough for me to fit inside.

I poked my nose and whiskers into the opening at the end of a roll, just to be sure I could fit myself in, and one sniff told me that I was not the only creature who had found this tunnel. A rat had been here before me—and might still be inside! I jerked my head out and leapt up on top of the fabric—no easy feat, as the cloth was very large around, but I'd found that my haunches were growing stronger every day, and I could now jump quite high when I had a mind to.

The cloth felt lovely under my paws, and I longed to sink my claws into it! Nothing on board the *Melissa Rae* was soft, save for the chairs in the captain's quarters and the lovely piece of calico that Melissa had given us, which I still slept on every night. But tempting as it was to dig my claws into these soft fabrics, I knew that they needed to be kept clean for delivery to New York and sale, so I resisted the urge. I remembered overhearing a conversation the captain had had with Moses one night, worrying over the cargo we were carrying:

"Without Mrs. Tibbs aboard, we'll be lucky to get those cottons to the States in one piece. Those rats below will tear through and make their nests in no time," the captain said, shaking his head.

"Not if young Jacob has a go at 'em," Moses said optimistically, and looked up from where he was at work changing the captain's bandages. "I think he'll make a fine mouser—you'll see." The captain gave me a sad look, and I could tell he wished that Moses's words would make it true.

Looking at the huge bolts of cloth, I understood now the captain's worries. The cotton would make a lovely home for any animal—cat or rat—and it was my job to keep it safe and whole. I climbed up a roll, front paws latching into the cotton but gently, as to not leave tears, and made my way to the top roll of fabric on the pile.

I walked its length and made a quick inspection—the cloth still looked whole and unsullied. But the smell I had picked up along the bottom rolls left me worried. Were rats nesting there, tearing into the fabric and making it their own? I decided that this was where I must stand vigil and wait for the vermin to make their mistake.

I got my wits about me and leapt down to one of the large wooden crates placed tight up against the bolts of cloth. I landed, front paws first, and sniffed the crate's strange, metallic smell. These crates were positioned to hold the large bolts of cloth in place (for otherwise they would roll about the boat), but they also contained goods that we were bringing to America—muskets with black barrels and large pistols, along with the gunpowder to work them. The muskets were packed ten and twenty to a crate, and we had almost three hundred aboard.

Other crates were carrying mail and packages that people from Liverpool and surrounding towns wanted sent to the Americas. I had heard the sailors talking about the *Melissa Rae* as a "packet" ship, meaning that she was hired to carry packages across the Atlantic. And she did. In fact, until the captain sold his boat to Archer's Shipping Company, he had set his own sailing schedule. He'd been free to leave port when he wanted to, when his ship was full, to make as much or as little as he desired on each trip. But as part of the Archer line, he would leave when the company scheduled a departure, whether the hold was full or not. From the looks of things below, the ship would make quite a profit on this trip—and that would be increased depending on how quickly we made the crossing. Being a dependable and fast ship meant more money for the company and a bonus for the captain, which he would share with his sailors. In essence, the captain was racing against himself and the *Melissa Rae*'s best time across—always striving for faster, and to arrive with unsullied goods.

We were also carrying lead and iron, things that were made in England and were needed in America. There were two tons of lead in small bars and thousands of copper rods on board. The crates containing these were heavy, and once they were loaded to, they would not move again—no matter how strong a storm or gale we weathered—until we reached the shore.

At dinner one night I had heard Chippy complaining that this type of shipment weighed the *Melissa Rae* down—that we would not make our time and the bonus was out of reach. After Chippy left the galley that night, Archer called him a "packet rat"—a not-very-nice name for a sailor who usually hires out to work on packets. From what I'd heard, packet rats were rough and dirty men who cared for little aside from making a profit—they showed no loyalty. I knew Chippy to be a harsh fellow, but he was no packet rat. The only rats on this ship were right here in the hold with me.

I hunkered down atop the crate and kept my eyes wide,

to take in what little light made its way down to the hold. As I waited, my mind began to drift to odd things, and I found myself wondering about rats' eyes—could the hideous creatures see in the dark as well? They must, if they chose to live in the hold, I reasoned. This was what I was mulling when I spied a dark creature moving on the wooden planks near the bottom of the pile of cloth rolls. He would walk a few steps, then stop and sniff the air, walk a bit more, then do the same, putting his pointed nose up, his whiskers twitching. Had he picked up my scent as I had his?

I backed away from the edge of the crate so that he could not see me, but kept him in my own vision. As he neared the roll of cloth, I crouched down; my body seemed to know instinctively what to do. I readied myself to leap, the muscles in my haunches twitching. Then my back legs launched me, and all at once I was in the air, then atop the rat himself! I jumped back, perhaps as surprised and frightened as the rat was—now what would come of this?

The rat retreated, easing toward the tunnel in the cloth as I stalked forward. If he went into the hole, I would not follow him, for I was too afraid of the dark, confined space and the rat's horrible teeth, which he showed me now with a wet hiss as his thin, furless tail slashed the air behind him like a whip. Could this be, I wondered, the same rat from the galley? If so, this gray monster looked even bigger now than he had before, and perhaps I, too, looked larger to him, as the soup Moses had been sneaking to me had helped me to fill out a bit.

I stealthily put one paw in front of the other, slowly making my way toward the rat; our eyes were locked in a hatred that made the hair on my back stand up straight. As I crept forward, keeping my belly low to the ground, I heard a low, deep growl escape my throat that I had never heard myself make before—it scared even me! But for every step I took, he took another one, moving backward toward his escape.

I readied myself again, coiling up all my energy into my haunches, then pounced—I had him! His head was beneath my paw, and his fat belly rolled upright, exposed for my teeth to sink into. Before I could even think what to do next, I felt a tug at my leg—he was snapping at me with his horrible teeth, trying to bite. He opened his mouth wide to bite down, and I saw a patch of yellow and white fur—my own!—trapped in his giant teeth. I jerked away my paw, instinctively, before he could get hold of my leg, and bounded back. The rat jumped to his feet, now freed, and stared at me with his runny yellow eyes.

I stood stock-still and glared at my hated foe, and he returned my stare. He moved to circle around me, slowly sidestepping, and I did the same. Then he stopped and reversed direction, and so I followed, each of us mirroring the other, back and forth. Then something sounded behind me—a metal clink—and I turned to glance over my shoulder. A serious mistake. When I looked back round,

I had missed my chance—the gray rat spun fast and disappeared into the roll of cotton cloth before I could move. It was over, my first fight: a draw.

I made my way to the top of the roll of fabric as soon as I knew he was gone, and counted my blessings. I licked the spot on my leg where he had torn a tuft of fur and found that it didn't hurt much, though he'd left me with a round bald patch. My pride was far more wounded than my leg.

It took me a few moments to catch my breath and try to reason out what had happened. I should have leapt on him differently, holding his jaws closed as I made my attack. I should have used both paws. And if I had not been distracted by that sound—nothing more than the sailors putting down something metal on the deck overhead—perhaps I could have done him in. Next time, I told myself, I would know better, and things would be different.

I kept watch from the top of the roll of cloth for an hour, perhaps more, but no other rats came. Maybe they had heard or seen the fight with the Gray One and were staying away? I continued to run the fight over and over in my head as I lay there waiting, thinking about how I would do it differently if given the chance, until my tired body fell into a light nap and I rested.

When I awoke, it took a moment or two to remember where I was: sleeping atop a roll of cloth in the hold. I moved to stretch my legs out long, careful not to dig too deeply into the fabric with my claws, and to arch my back. I was at work straightening out my fur and whiskers before heading back up to deck when a quick shadow caught my eye—a rat below me! I crouched; my mind felt barely awake, but my body was ready to attack. This rat was not the same one—he was a bit smaller, quicker, and black instead of gray. But he, too, had that funny way of walking, then stopping to sniff the air. Maybe it was just when they got close to me that they sniffed about like this? The rat stopped just below where I perched and sniffed the air this way and that. Then he came up on his hind legs, his front legs raised, paws hanging down, and turned his head up, his whiskers and nose twitching. He turned to the right, and that's when he laid his beady eyes upon me.

As his eyes locked on mine, I only had a moment to see fear in his little face before I leapt and was all at once atop him! I brought his body to the floor with a hard thump as I landed, his hindquarters held with my left paw and his face under my right. Without even thinking what to do, I brought my teeth down and bit into his belly. He let out a high-pitched sound, and I tasted something in my mouth—warm and salty. Blood. I lifted my head, standing over him as he squirmed under my paws, crying in pain. What now? He was still alive, and in terrible pain. How could I actually kill the beast? I didn't want him to suffer as he was, but I was uncertain how to end it as he twisted this way and that.

I looked to the place where his head met his body and, mustering my courage, went in for a bite there. My teeth met something hard, and it crunched as I bit down harder and shook my head from side to side. It took only a second, maybe two; then his body was limp. There was no struggle, no sound. I lifted my paws off him gingerly and shook them, as if he were a dirty puddle I had stepped in. The black rat lay in front of me, his limbs loose, his mouth slightly open as if he were asleep. But his head was at that funny angle, turned in an unnatural way that to me, since seeing Slattery's body the night of the storm, would always signal death.

I must have stood there panting and looking at the rat for some time before I realized what I had done: I had *killed* him. I had done what the captain wanted of me, and what my mother had done for years before I had ever been born. I tried to connect the memory of my beloved mother with the scene before me, and I could not. I could not picture her biting, clawing another creature, taking its life. It was a side of her that I had not chanced to see, and I found it very hard to believe.

I wondered if she would be proud of me, as I picked up the dark rat by the scruff of his neck and made my way to the ladder that would lead me back to the main deck. I was exhausted, sore, and somewhat sad about what had transpired. The sound of the rat's cry still rang in my ears. I questioned if I had done the right thing, the right way. But I also now had something to leave outside the captain's door—just as my mother had done—and in my proud little body there was no room for doubt. So I pushed those feelings aside and focused only on the plan I had made to save the captain. I would lay this rat outside his door and I would wait. When he awoke, he would see it. And then he would be well.

When I arrived on the deck, my prize in my mouth, I was surprised that it was not still night. Bright sunlight washed over the deck. I had been below for some time, but how long? I made my way to the captain's cabin and dropped the rat outside his door. Then I lay down, nesting my head in my front paws. I could not stop a deep purr from rising in my throat—how excited I was! Finally I had earned my keep aboard the *Melissa Rae*, and I meant to continue to do so. I closed my eyes, just for a moment, and played back the fight over and over again in my mind.

"What's this?" I heard Moses say, waking me from my light sleep. I roused myself to look up into his surprised face. "Jacob, is this your work?" His eyes went to the dead rat, and for a moment I doubted that he was pleased. Then I realized that he was teasing me, when with a wink he opened the door and announced to the captain what I had accomplished. I could hear the captain talking inside, but I was too embarrassed to take a look within—my appearance must be dreadful, with my bald tuft on my foreleg and my fur askew. Instead I stood outside and waited.

Moses came out at last with a weak smile on his face. "He's terribly proud of you," he said, petting me down my back. "Not feeling much better today, though." Moses stood and stopped for a second, taking a step back. "My, you are becoming a real young fellow, aren't you? Handsome as can be, the spit and image of your mother."

He smiled, and from the look in his eye I could tell that he, too, was remembering my mother and perhaps thinking how proud she would be of me now. His kind words were enough to encourage me to rouse myself, take a wet paw to my face, and begin my day.

CHAPTER 13

A WARRIOR'S WAY

When you are a sailor, and I now considered myself one, the days at sea begin to pass in a most ordinary way. If the weather is "shipshape"—clear and a good wind—you cannot tell a Monday from a Wednesday, or any other day. The sunrise and sunset come and go in a predictable pattern that somewhat bored me. I could not fathom how the sailors could repeat the same tasks and eat the same boring meals every day, day in and day out.

Waking in the gray light of the early-morning bells, I would tumble from my cozy spot in the galley and go up to watch the sun rise. I always stood for a moment at the stern, to take in the color of the morning sky and wait for any odd feelings, like those I had on the morning of the terrible storm. I planted my feet firmly and closed my eyes, breathing in the sea air. But I did not again get that awful, foreboding emotion that would predict a storm.

Sadly, I did not have the power to recognize that another type of storm would eventually engulf us all.

Following early-morning bells, the sailors would start their day scrubbing down the boards with sloppy seawater and lye soap. They would raise and lower sails according to the wind, repair anything that wanted fixing, and spend their idle time working on the ropes. When there seemed no more work to be done, there was the tedious task of picking oakum—taking apart old slacks of rope, bit by bit—to use around the ship, stuffing joints and leaks.

One day, with the real work of the ship behind them, the fellows were sitting on the hot, sunny deck with a pile of oakum and decided to have a bit of fun. As I played nearby with a stray piece of string, thrown to me by one of the men, they took me into their confidence and spoke to me as a fellow mate. I can now understand that the sailors were as bored as I, and needed something to set their minds to. "Archer has an affliction to this cat," Chippy said, watching me bat the string to and fro across the deck with my paw. "What if he were to wake and find the creature in his own bunk?"

I could see Sean's brown eyes sparkling at the idea. "Do you mean to put Jacob—accidentally, of course—into his quarters?" he asked.

A young sailor named Daly joined in the fun, whispering, "Not just his quarters—into the bunk itself, the bedding and all!"

The three men moved toward me, and before I could

leap, Chippy's large, rough hand closed around my middle. They crept to Archer's quarters, all the while watching to be sure the man himself was not on deck but remained below, having tea in the galley. Sean pulled open the door and glanced quickly inside, and Chippy placed me gently onto a small, short bed, much like what the captain had in his room, only these quarters were a bit tighter.

"Roll around there, Jacob; get a good feel for it." Sean laughed as I set my nails into the soft bedding, kneading it under my paws. I did not fully understand their intentions, but as my kneading seemed to please the sailors so much, I did it a bit more. Sean clapped and rubbed his hands together. "That's it."

"You make yourself at home there, rat," Chippy said, and petted me roughly on the back as they turned to leave. And then I was alone in the dark quarters on soft bedding. I kneaded the blanket below me until I had raised some threads, making it even softer, though perhaps not as attractive as it had been. Then I waited a while, but when Chippy and Sean didn't return, there seemed to be nothing better to do than curl up and have a rest. And that is indeed what I did, right on the middle of the softest bit, which I later learned was Archer's own pillow.

I cannot say what time passed, as I usually did not heed the ringing bells that would signal the hour, but when I woke it was to the hollering of Archer and his stamping boot. Quite a rude awakening! "Out, you vermin. Out this instant!" he yelled, his jacket buttons undone, exposing a stained white shirt and a round belly

that pushed against it. Archer would not touch me; as I had learned quickly on, I repulsed him. But instead he waved his hands furiously over my body as I slowly stretched my length on his pillow, easing my muscles out of the deep sleep that I had enjoyed on his soft bed.

He turned to a side table and took up a leather-bound book, swatting at me as if I were an insect. "Go on then, you! Go out!" He pulled open the door to his quarters and pushed me off the bed with the book, shoving my bottom as I reluctantly made my way out onto the wooden deck. "Go, you arrogant beast!"

The sunny deck was a hard adjustment for my eyes, so while I did exit his room, I lay down on the deck in front of his door to gather my wits, but the man kept after me, shoving and pushing, now with his boot. "You are not welcome here—go, and take your fleas with you!"

As I did finally make my way down to the deck, I noted that the sailors had all suspended their work and were watching the proceedings with eagerness. Even Chippy and Sean, who should have been below, were on deck to witness Archer's red face and sudden sneezing fit. The man doubled over, again and again, *achoo*ing and wheezing between yelling and swatting, before he finally tumbled back into his quarters, holding his chest. Even with the door closed behind him, we could hear the respiratory ailments that continued to afflict him.

The sailors hardly waited to see his door close before the laughter started. Chippy and Sean exchanged satisfied looks, and I continued my path through the sailors, enjoying the congratulatory pets along my back and cheers of "Good on you, Jacob!"

It was at times such as these when I felt the most closely bonded with the sailors—and missed my mother most fervently. A good number of the crew, and I among them, held Archer more than partially responsible for my mother's death and that of young Slattery, as it was at Archer's urging that we sailed directly into the storm. So while it may have appeared a bit of good ribbing to anger the man, there was a current of true animosity for Archer that ran just below the surface. Since the captain had been injured, Archer had been more than happy to step into the role of substitute captain—much to the chagrin of the sailors. If our first mate had been an experienced man, such as Sean or Chippy, the men would not have minded a lick. But Archer's lack of experience, combined with his arrogance, led him to continually make a spectacle of himself. He was not in favor with the men. So I could not blame them for having a bit of fun. If anything, their exploits had broken up the boring routine of daily life aboard the *Melissa Rae*, and I welcomed a change from the usual.

Even the grub that Moses served the men was the same every day: breakfast was a gruel of water and oatmeal with coffee to wash it down; lunch was usually hardtack biscuits with a bite of meat—salt pork or beef—and dinner was fish-head soup, maybe fried corn porridge, potatoes, or pickles. On the Sabbath, however, Moses made a special treat: a batch of pudding with molasses, called duff, which the sailors adored but I could not abide.

I had no way of marking the time except to note that I was, indeed, growing larger and stronger every day. I was still a kitten, to be sure, but my paws appeared larger, even to me, and I had to squeeze myself quite flat to fit beneath the warm stove in the galley. Every day, I checked the galley pantry and the ship's food supply. To have a nest of rats there would be quite terrible for all on board. And every night, I went below, searching for my enemies and keeping tabs on the goods in the hold, looking for damage or any signs of habitation. I did not find a foe on every night, but when I did, I was quick about things. I went for the neck before the creature even had a moment to cry out in pain. When I was done, I would carry whatever I had caught up to the deck, and lay the bodies outside the captain's door by dawn.

On one particular morning, when I had caught two rats—albeit small ones—I went to lay my prizes outside his quarters and realized I'd not seen the captain in many days. How many to be exact, I could not be sure, but his progress, or lack, had been unchecked by me. So later, when the last meal of the day had been served, I was close at Moses's heels when he made his way up to the captain's cabin with the brown bottle in hand.

The room was dark and smelled musty, but there was the captain, lying stretched out on the divan, as he had been the last time I had visited him. He gave a weak whistle for me, and I leapt up by his side. He seemed pleased to see me. "My boy, how are you?" He scratched me under my chin, and I surprised myself to hear a deep, loud purr escape my throat. "I hear that you are growing up to be a fine ratter," the captain said, his voice quiet and gravelly.

"Aye, that he is, sir," Moses agreed, taking a seat in the chair beside him. "He brings up one or two a day now. How do you fare tonight?" He started to unwrap the stained bandages over the captain's wounded leg, and a terrible smell escaped. I knew what that smell was. The first rat I had left outside the captain's door, the one that had sat in the heat of the sun for a day, had given off the same terrible stink as its body swelled up and collected flies. Dougherty eventually tossed it overboard, before the captain had even had a chance to see it. "Good job, mate," he called to me as I watched him carry the rat's bloated body to the side of the ship, holding it gingerly by its tail. "But these vermin aren't for collecting!" The planks where it had lain gave off a bad smell until the decks were washed down the next morning. Now I was terrified to witness the same smell again. Did this mean the captain would die?

I heard Moses pull in a deep breath and let out a sigh as he wrapped the leg back up. "'Tis not good, Captain. Worse now than ever. I know you'll disagree, but I have to put forth again that we talk to Archer and chance turning back."

"Preposterous," the captain snapped. He pushed Moses's hands away and did the rewrapping himself. I'd not seen him so angry since after the storm, when he had given Archer a stern talking-to. "It will heal, or it will not. I cannot ask my crew to make a fool's errand of returning an ailing captain to port."

"Sir, I worry that it is too late for an amputation. A wound like this might be poisoning your blood. I've seen it before—"

"With all due respect, man," the captain barked, "you are no doctor!"

Moses kept his calm. "I am not a doctor, sir, that is correct. And that is indeed why I would ask you to let us return you to England so that you can see one. Before it becomes too—"

"You are dismissed," the captain said, turning his head away from us both. "Leave the bottle," he added as Moses stood. I kept my place beside the captain and nudged his side with my head, rubbing my ears against him. "You too, Jacob. Go now. I'm not fit for company." The captain's voice sounded weak again, so I did as he asked and leapt down, scooting out the open door before Moses closed it behind him.

I followed Moses back to the galley, and I noted that he stopped along the way twice, once to rouse Sean from his hammock and again to lean in on Chippy during his poker game. To both of them he said the same thing: "It is time."

The second and third mates followed the cook into the galley, and I knew that I could easily have stayed and hidden beneath the stove, listening to every word. But the sight of the captain and the smell in his cabin had made me feel restless, useless in a way I could hardly stand. I could not, would not, accept that the captain would go the way of my mother and sailor Slattery, tossed overboard like a dead and bloated rat! I would not allow it. I would do the only thing I knew: go below and do my job. The sailors had said that when my mother lined up dead vermin outside the captain's door, it put a smile on his face. So now I would do the same. I would beat her record, and either I would make him well again or his last day on board would be one where he was the most pleased and proud of the runt he had saved, of Mr. Jacob Tibbs.

As I crossed back over the deck to the main hatch, I sensed a change on board: a certain tightness had taken hold. The sailors seemed more subdued to me; there was less chatter in the second dogwatch, just the men going about their business with little of the jovial nature that was usually evident. It might have been my imagination, but I thought I heard whispers as I scurried down the hatch, set on achieving my goal by the time daylight broke over the waves. Perhaps this whispering had been going on for some time and I had not taken notice of it. Perhaps it was new tonight, with word of the ailing captain. I focused my eyes on the darkness around me. The captain had given me only one task on this ship, and I was determined to do it.

The first kill that night came easily. I was well rested and eager, and found a small rat who'd wandered into the wrong place at the wrong time. Perhaps I was growing faster, more agile, or perhaps my reputation among the rats was beginning to be known, because when I made eyes on the kill, the little rat froze in place and I was upon him in a blink. I laid the limp body at the bottom of the ladder to take up later. I noted he was indeed small, but still a rat. Not bad, I reasoned, not bad.

But my early luck on this night was not to be repeated. I prowled the hold in the dark and quiet for hours, not coming across any other vermin, until I grew tired. I hopped up on a wooden trunk and spread my body the length of it, digging my nails into the wood for a nice stretch, then curled into a ball. I would close my eyes, not for long—it took but a few moments to wake and feel refreshed again. A "catnap," one of the sailors had called it, though you wouldn't find any of them taking such a rest, not while on watch. Just two days previous, one young sailor had tried to grab a rest under the longboat when all was shipshape during his watch. When Archer found him, he grew so angry you would think someone had poured hot tar on his head. He screamed and went red in the face, telling the sailor and anyone else who would listen that this type of behavior was unacceptable. He ordered the young sailor to remain on deck for the next two watches without a rest or meal between. Punishment served, the poor lad had stumbled to his hammock, dead on his feet, and since then I'd always seen him at his best on the deck, never slacking on a watch again. He had learned his lesson.

When I'd been resting for what felt like only a few

minutes but may have been a quarter bell, I heard a slight sound and my ears perked. It was quiet below, aside from the gentle sounds of the waves against the side of the ship and occasional footfalls above, but I'd grown used to those and knew the noises well. This was something else.

I opened my eyes and slowly turned my head—to move too quickly might scare whoever, or whatever, was near. It didn't take me long to spot the source of the noise: a large gray rat was gnawing away on the wooden pin inside a roll of cloth. One of the sailors had said that rats' teeth continued to grow, and that was why they constantly had to chew and gnaw at hard things, to sand down their long, horrible front teeth. The scraping sound was subtle but had been loud enough to wake me. I quickly got my wits about me and moved onto my paws without a sound. At least, I thought I hadn't made a sound. But the rat stopped and turned its head ever so slowly, looking over the shoulder and directly at me.

It was the Gray One. The one I had met in the galley, then again in the hold. My first battle. I would know that terrible face anywhere: the huge top teeth, the piercing eyes. And now I would have my revenge. The thought of leaving this huge rat's body outside the captain's door was enough to boost my bravery. The rat hissed quietly, a warning. We were now about the same size—a very small cat and a very big rat. The battle would be somewhat more even—yes, the rat had his wretched teeth, but I had my claws. And I also had a taste for vengeance and a victory for the captain to achieve. Tonight I would be unbeatable.

When my stare did not waver, the Gray One turned and scurried down the narrow path between two rolls of cloth. I leapt and followed him in a heartbeat, close enough to nip at his tail if I'd chosen to. When the path ended and we found ourselves on the other side of the hold, the rat paused, unsure of where to go next, while I crouched to leap. If he stood still for even a moment, he was mine. It was dark below, but my eyes were fast to see in the murk, and I'd learned the stockpiles here well—I now knew my way through these barrels, stacks, and trunks by heart. Then he made a fatal mistake: the Gray One leapt over a wooden chest, and I knew that on the other side was nothing but wall, and that I would at last have him cornered. The biggest rat I'd seen aboard! How proud I would make the captain in the morn. I could hardly wait to see his face.

I leapt down and made to pounce, forcing him back into a corner from where he could not escape. He scampered backward, then would go no farther, standing his ground and hissing, showing me his big yellow teeth. I crouched low and felt my back legs twitch, muscles ready to pounce . . . and then I saw something move behind him.

Something small—no, there was more than one.

A rat's nest! This was home, and those tiny gray fur balls were babies. There must have been eight, maybe ten of them, each no bigger than one of my paws, their little eyes not yet open. Smelling their mother, one of them set to squeaking, begging for food. The Gray One hissed again and backed up a bit more, now standing over her nest tucked in the corner. And he was indeed a *she*—this giant rat that I had feared since my first days aboard was a female! Her young ones nudged her underbelly to nurse, completely unaware of the danger I posed to their mother, and to them.

If I took her now, which I could do easily, they would die here in the course of a day or two, starved to death. I paused, then took a step back, then two. I could not do to those creatures what had been done to me, even if they were my sworn enemies. In time they would grow and be worthy adversaries, but now they were innocents, too young to be a part of this fight. I eased backward, keeping my eyes locked on hers, then leapt onto the wooden box and picked my way over the parcels, heading for the deck. I would rest there, by the captain's door, until the sky grew light again.

I had taken only one rat, not my mother's record—not even close—but still I thought she would have been proud of the choice I made, and I felt her warm blessing in my chest as I slipped through the hole and breathed in the fresh night air, the stars bright and shining on the wooden planks that I now knew by heart, my home.

CHAPTER 14

MUTINY

While I had been below in the hold overnight, the mood aboard the *Melissa Rae* had changed. It was not so much what was said, but more what wasn't. I noted early the next morning that the sailors were not happy and jovial going about their tasks. There was not the usual ribbing and teasing, and absent were the songs and smiles that commonly greeted me as I sat outside the captain's quarters. I would soon learn why. There was a disagreement on board, and stubborn anger was brewing. On one side were Moses and the captain's trusted mates, who wanted to turn back to Liverpool in order to save the captain's life. On the other side were Archer and a few of the other sailors—Daly, Dougherty, and Smyth among them—who wanted to keep on course.

Being on a ship for a long spell, I've learned, is a strange thing indeed. Confined, as we are, to a small space and with only each other for company, men find their tempers begin to rise, and even little slights—one sailor getting an extra biscuit or cup of tea—can escalate into a true disagreement that boils over. I had heard, in the galley and on deck, sailors grumbling about each other and about the captain's condition. Gossip and speculation, anger over extra shifts and Archer's favoritism, foul insults of Moses's meager cooking skills—these all spilled over and swirled into an angry mess of talk.

With the ringing of eight bells at noon for the afternoon watch, a meeting was called on deck with Sean yelling, "All hands!" Sleeping night-watch sailors tumbled up to the deck and stood outside the captain's quarters, grumbling. The sailors who were now on watch dropped their ropes and soapy brushes and also made their way to stand in two lines. I had remained curled in a ball outside the captain's quarters for most of the morning bells—my one measly kill from the night before beside me—waiting for the captain to acknowledge my work. Usually by this time of the day, Moses would have been on deck, bringing the captain a bite and tallying my kills from the night before. But on this day, he had not yet arrived and I wondered at the change in schedule. Now I roused myself and tried to tidy my fur quickly. I could tell from the quiet and solemn faces among the sailors that something serious was afoot.

"What is the meaning of this?" Archer stumbled out to the quarterdeck, leaving his room as he rarely did during the day. After the captain's accident and illness, the command of the ship had fallen to him, as first mate. But he had been happy to let Sean and Chippy run the *Melissa*

Rae while he sat in an overstuffed armchair in his quarters, reading from a leather-bound book. He seemed to think that that was the job of a captain—to do nothing while others worked. The rest of us usually laid eyes on him only at mealtimes. Now he stood before us, his shirt untucked and his greasy hair uncombed. "I am first mate, may I remind you, and I've not called for all hands." His mean little eyes met Sean's warm brown ones as they stood beside each other next to the bell.

Sean turned to address the sailors without responding to Archer. "There has been talk, above and below, of the captain's condition. As we are all aware, he is gravely ill." Sean's eyes went to Moses, who removed his hat and crumpled it to his chest, looking down. "Can you report further, Cook?"

The small man had tears brewing when he looked up, and I knew at once that the captain was no more. That was why he had not congratulated me on last night's kill, why the door to his quarters had not opened all day . . .

"He's had a turn these past days, and is as sick as any man can be and still be called living," Moses said quietly. But I feared he was not telling the whole truth. Was the captain still with us?

Sean nodded and went on: "We are almost three weeks out, with another three to reach America—that is, with perfect conditions, more than we can hope to expect. But if we return now to port, turning today—"

And here Archer cut him off: "This is foolish talk—nonsense! What difference does it make if the man spends his last days coming or going? He'll not survive either way."

Some of the men nodded in agreement, but Sean continued to explain his point. "The west-to-east currents are faster: a return should take no more than fourteen days—and with this crew, and the captain's life at stake, I expect we would do better than that."

"Aye, ten days!" Chippy barked out, and a few of the men cheered him, willing to take on the challenge of racing back to Liverpool.

Archer walked across the quarterdeck, his hands clasped behind his back, looking down. He stopped beside me and nudged the dead rat with his black boot, his eyes meeting mine for a brief moment. "And what then?" He looked up into the faces of the men. "We arrive back in Liverpool in fourteen—or ten—days' time, as you say, most likely with a dead man aboard who was once your captain, and a hold full of undelivered goods. Goods for which we have collected no fees." He stopped pacing and looked at the men. "Do you expect that the Archer Shipping Company will gladly dole out the coins, pay you your wages, and you will all toddle off the docks and go home to your loved ones?" His voice dripped with sarcasm.

The sailors looked from one to another and realized what he was saying. There would be no pay, after spending over a month at sea. In fact they would be in debt to the shipping company for room and board, and the likelihood of another job aboard any ship—not just an Archer ship—would be slim.

"I say we press on: it's what the captain would have wanted," Archer said calmly. "We sail through to New York Harbor. The captain's health is not my concern."

Sean stepped forward to speak, but Archer cut him off, putting a hand to his chest. "You will hold your tongue, second mate, or I will lower your rank! Now dismiss these men and go about your business."

I stood quietly at the feet of the two men, just outside the captain's door, wondering what, if any, of the argument the captain had heard.

"I respectfully refuse your order," Sean replied. "I will not dismiss these men, not until a vote has been had. A vote to see who among them would return to Liverpool, and who would push on." Sean towered over the smaller man and looked down at him now, waiting for a response.

Archer stood his ground, his eyes narrowing. "Yes, I second your idea—let's have a vote," he spat out. He turned back to the men. "All those in favor of a return to Liverpool on this watch, say 'aye' and raise your right hand."

The men stood silently, in two lines. Most kept their eyes down, inspecting their own bare feet or the boards of the deck. The sound of the canvas sails in the wind and the soft, rhythmic clunk of the waves against the ship were the only sounds to be heard.

"Not one of you?" Archer scoffed, glancing at the second mate.

"Aye," Sean spoke first, raising his hand, his eyes locked on Archer's.

Chippy followed, raising his right hand by his chest. "Aye," he boomed in his deep voice.

"Aye." Bobby Doyle stepped forward, the youngest sailor on the *Melissa Rae* other than myself. He proudly raised his hand.

Moses lifted his three-pointed hat back to his bald head and spoke clearly: "Aye."

The other sailors stood quietly. Dougherty sniffled but kept his eyes down, while Smyth glanced cautiously around, as if nervous. A rope slapped the main mast in a sad echo, catching the wind. Archer waited a full moment more before asking, "Is that *all* of you, then? Four men, out of a full crew?"

The men who had raised their hands stood in place, heads up, defiant even in the face of a losing vote. "Dougherty, you are now first mate. Please escort these four to the hold, where they will serve the remainder of this journey." Archer spoke quickly, turning on his heel.

"What's that?" Dougherty asked, confused. The other sailors looked to each other, unable to make sense of what had just happened.

Archer turned back to the men, speaking in a stately way. "If the captain is truly unconscious, as Moses reports, then I, as first mate, am now the captain. These men are guilty of planning a mutiny against me, and I will not abide it!" As he spoke, his voice grew louder, his face redder. He paced the quarterdeck above the men, and as he neared me, his boot almost caught my underside.

"Pardon, sir," Dougherty began to say.

"You will take them to the hold and lock them in, until such time as I have decided on their punishment." Archer reached swiftly into his jacket pocket and came out with something black in his hand. The men cowered at the sight of it, and, as I watched with curiosity, he waved it over his head. "Do as you are ordered, first mate!"

"Aye, sir." Dougherty looked cautiously at the black object in Archer's hand—a gun, I now saw, which was pointed directly at him—and moved to Chippy. "Come, I've no choice in the matter."

Chippy looked at Dougherty and scowled, shoving the bigger man back. "You're a coward," he spat. He looked to his friends around him, fellow sailors he had known and traveled with for years. "You're all cowards! You'd let this mouse of a man push on for profit, and cost us the life of Captain Natick?"

Dougherty moved quickly this time, around Chippy, pulling his arms behind him to hold him tight. But Chippy was faster still, spinning to strike the man in the face with a closed fist. It all happened in a flash, and then blood was pouring from Dougherty's nose and all down his front. His hand went to his face and came away with bloody fingers. You could almost see steam come off his shoulders from his brewing anger.

Dougherty's bloody hands went round Chippy's neck, two big, meaty paws encircling his throat as if to choke the life from him. Chippy reached up to claw at Dougherty's hands, but the former fighter was too strong: Chippy's face began to redden, then turn crimson. It was a terrifying scene—our two biggest sailors in a tussle! There was not a man on the ship strong enough to pull them apart, and I felt sure one would gravely injure the other. I crouched, ready to leap onto Dougherty's back and sink my claws in to loosen his grip on Chippy's throat, but before I could move, Archer stepped in front of me. He motioned into the sky over the sails and pulled back his arm, eliciting a huge boom and a rain of hot sparks. Black smoke filtered down, and a smell I recognized from the barrels stored below in the hold: gunpowder.

"Cease!" Archer yelled into the mess of men now piled on the deck, wrestling each with the other. It was as if they had all been waiting for just the right moment to bring out their grievances in physical form. They stood and brushed themselves off, Dougherty wiping with the back of a hand at his nose, which still dripped red blood like a broken barrel of dark wine.

"Again, I order you to kindly remove these four men and enclose them in the hold. Or I will end them here, one by one." He waved the pistol in front of the sailors. Standing so close to him, I could see that his hand, as it held the large black gun, was shaking. Even with the weapon he was a scared, soft man.

Then, from behind me, through the captain's door, I heard something, faintly. Someone calling. It was the captain! The sound of the commotion and the gunshot had been enough to wake him. I heard him let out a whistle for me, and I raced to the wooden door and set my claws into it, digging furiously. I had to reach him.

A hand closed about my middle, pulling me back while my claws were still engaged, and I found myself flying through the air, tossed as if a bag of flour. I landed on all four paws on the deck, digging in to steady myself. I looked up to see Archer standing behind me, a sickening grin on his face. "And don't forget to take that animal with them," he hissed, turning on his heel and returning to his quarters without a backward glance.

CHAPTER 15

PRISONERS

Though I had never had trouble weaving my way in and out of the iron bars that lined either side of the hold, the men were too big to slip through. So that was where Dougherty and Smyth brought us, Sean carrying me in the crook of his arm, and locked us up tight. The bars were in place to hold cargo steady, and that they did, on either end of the ship. So filled was the space with all the packages, there was no footing here for man or cat, no open floor at all. So we sat, perching atop the many crates and cases that were shipping to America.

"If we had any more light, I could see the barrels of gunpowder and the chest of pistols I know is stored down here," Sean grumbled, scratching his bushy beard. He was not correct, though, as I knew those items to be stored in the center of the hold and on the bow side, not here in the stern, where they were now trapped.

"What would you do with those, if you could get hold

of them?" Moses asked. "The captain always says it's a weak man who turns to gunpowder to do his work for him."

I leapt down from Sean's lap and slid between the bars to the main section of the hold, sniffing about for vermin, as was my habit. The men took no notice of me, so worried were they over their own predicament.

"If the captain does wake, and hears of this . . . ," Chippy started.

Sean let out a light laugh. "Oh, I wouldn't want to be Archer when that man awakes! He'd make a cat-o'-nine sing against his back."

"But what chance of that?" Bobby asked. His young face in the dim light looked so innocent and childlike. "What's the chance the captain might be all right?" I turned and paced back to the men, eager to hear what Moses might answer.

Moses shook his head. "I wish I could say otherwise, but the captain will likely not wake."

Chippy shifted on the crate where he was sitting and brought his palm down hard, cursing. "And you should be tending him, not caged up down here!"

Moses looked over at the large man and tried to calm him. "Don't raise bile over it, Chip; he's past all that. His soul is in God's hands now—there is no difference tending can make."

The men fell silent, each thinking his own thoughts and perhaps offering prayers for the health of their captain. We were there for only a handful of hours before a lantern came down the main hatch and moved toward us in the darkness. I expected to see Archer's face, but instead it was another sailor, the man called Daly.

"So I've come to let you up," he mumbled, fitting the key into the lock and swinging open the iron gate. He seemed unable—or unwilling—to meet the eyes of his former friends. "Archer wants a word."

As the men filed out, Daly closed the gate behind them and followed them across the hold and to the ladder. "And, mates, it's *Captain* Archer now," he whispered. "Or he'll go right mad."

I heard Chippy let out a laugh, and I knew he wouldn't be calling Archer his captain any time soon.

The men climbed up, and I was quick on the ladder rungs behind them. As soon as my paws reached the deck, I could tell there had been a change—not only in the temperament of the sailors, but in the whole of the ship and how she sailed. The *Melissa Rae* was not moving, the sails hung limp and heavy on their masts, and the air that surrounded us was thick and wet.

"'Tis the doldrums," Sean murmured, wiping sweat from his forehead.

"You will not speak unless spoken to!" Archer yelled down at him from the quarterdeck. The other sailors had no work to do in this still phase of wind, so they sat, sweating and rumpled with sour faces, lined up along the gunwale at the starboard side of the ship, watching to see how Archer handled the situation.

Archer grasped his hands behind his back, jutting his

round belly out. I noted he did this often, as if he had once seen a true captain pace on deck in this manner. It was not convincing. "This ship can have only one captain, and that is I. If you choose to obey me, you will return to your former rank—Sean, you will assume first mate and Chippy second. However, if you men choose to defy me, you will not only lose rank, but also be confined to the hold for the remainder of our journey."

"Mr. Archer, what if the captain comes to his wits?" young Bobby asked.

Archer's face reddened, and I watched as small drops of sweat seemed to bubble to the surface of his skin. He took the steps down from the quarterdeck and moved swiftly to the young man. We all watched as he slapped him, openhanded, across the cheek. "You will address me as Captain Archer!" he hollered.

The boy cowered and stepped back. I'd never heard tell of Captain Natick striking a man, and I doubted the sailors had either, from the looks on their faces. "You will all, to a one, address me as Captain Archer!"

"And if we will not?" Sean asked quickly.

"I will . . ." Archer brought his hand to his forehead, furiously wiping away perspiration. "I will put you and your lot out in the longboat."

"You cannot," Chippy scoffed gruffly. The other sailors began to talk, turning one to another.

"He's gone right mad, 'asn't he?" Smyth could be heard to say.

"Silence! It is maritime law, and I as the captain will do

it. You men will respect me; I will not have insubordination."

"I would like an audience with Captain Natick, as is my right. I signed articles to serve under him, not you, *Mister* Archer." Sean spoke bravely. He brushed past Archer, barely giving the man a sidelong glance as he headed to the quarterdeck and the captain's door.

As soon as his hand was on the knob, I was by his heels, wanting desperately to see my captain and how he fared. The room was dark, windows blacked by heavy shades, and an odor of rot hung in the air. I saw Sean recoil reflexively before moving forward in the dim light.

"Captain?" he whispered to the form on the daybed. There was no response.

I moved to a place beside the great man but was unwilling to leap up for further inspection lest I wake him from a restorative sleep. But Sean reached down and took his hand in his, then felt at the captain's neck for a moment before moving the back of his hand across his forehead. Sean's face was grim, his mouth set in a line beneath his thick mustache. He leaned down, putting his ear to the captain's mouth, listening for a sound of life.

He stood after a moment and looked down at the great man before he stepped back into the sunlight of the deck. I followed him but lingered in the doorway of the captain's cabin, eager to hear what he would report to the sailors.

"All hope is not lost," Sean said quietly, to himself. Then he spoke loudly, addressing his mates: "There is still time to save the captain's life, if we turn now. But every moment is crucial."

Archer came around the captain's quarters just then, and I could see he was holding his pistol. He waved the black gun about over his head, "Dougherty, and you, the tall one"—he motioned to Smyth—"ready the longboat for these mutineers!"

The sailors sat as if stunned by the antics of the short, fat man on the quarterdeck, waving a big gun. "*Obey* my orders, or you will join them!" Archer yelled. With that Dougherty and Smyth leapt to their feet and untied the longboat that sat, overturned, in the middle of the deck. After the loss of the jolly boats during the storm, this was the only boat left aboard. When it was flipped upright, I could see rows of wooden benches inside, and several oars tucked in. The men moved the boat over to the gunwale and lashed both stern and bow with sailor's knots. They lifted it to hang, just over the side of the *Melissa Rae,* above the water.

Little did I know then that this small craft would be my home on the waves for the next eleven days.

CHAPTER 16

THE LONGBOAT

The next events occurred so swiftly and violently that I hesitate to report them for fear of my honesty being questioned. But this is exactly as it transpired, and I can only explain the actions of the men aboard the *Melissa Rae* on that day as sea madness, or the doldrums taking full effect. I can testify that they were all good men, those who I knew well enough to pass judgment on, forced into a precarious position with no reliable leadership, and I assume they managed as best they could. Still, their decisions on that day would become their undoing, and their superstitions would come to truths.

Archer, waving his gun, forced Sean and Chippy to the bulwark railing of the ship and held them there.

"Not the boy," Sean said as Archer forced him over the edge of the *Melissa Rae* and into the longboat. "Don't put him out; he's practically still a child."

Archer looked back over his shoulder at the boy Sean

referred to, Bobby Doyle: his young face, his blond hair held back in a braid. He was a handsome lad, and I regret sorely what happened to him.

Archer seemed not to hear him. "You lot, get off!" He shoved with his left hand, pushing Chippy and Sean into the longboat. "The boy can stay—but your captain joins you. If you want so much to return to Liverpool with him, you shall have your wish—but not with the *Melissa Rae.*" As Bobby took his place among the other sailors, Archer turned and motioned to Dougherty. "Go gather Natick and put him aboard," he ordered. "And where is that measly little cook?"

"Here, sir." Moses stepped up, seemingly from nowhere. He had disappeared for a moment, but now was back on deck. I didn't have time to speculate about where he had gone, but it would be apparent soon.

"Get on with it!" Archer waved the gun at him, motioning to the longboat. Moses willingly climbed in, tucking his greatcoat about him. It did seem odd that the man was wearing a large coat in such warm, humid weather, but no one had a mind to question him.

Dougherty came out from the captain's quarters, behind where I now stood, and I watched as he stepped carefully from the quarterdeck, cradling the captain in his arms. The great man was pale and his skin waxy under the hot, hazy sun; his eyes did not open. Dougherty's face betrayed no emotion as he gently lifted the captain and laid him in the bottom of the longboat, between the other men.

"Lower away!" Archer yelled, and Dougherty and Smyth both took up the ropes. I stood frozen outside the captain's quarters for a moment, as if the shock of the situation had paralyzed my very paws. And then I leapt down to the main deck and, without thought, raced at Archer, climbing up his trouser leg as if he were a wooden mast, digging my claws in deep. I am not proud to admit that I dug and scratched like a wild animal.

I had not known that a man with a gun—especially a madman—is a dangerous thing, and learned all at once when a loud shot rang out so close to my ears that I could hardly make a sound for a moment or two. Then a hand roughly wrenched me from my hold, tearing out one of my claws to the quick in the process, and I was thrown with force upon the deck, the air pushed from my lungs.

"You miserable beast!" Archer yelled. Before I could scrabble away, he reached for me and lifted me by my neck, holding so tight I could not breathe and saw bright stars sprinkling through my vision. He held me up over the side of the ship, and in my delirious state I saw the longboat meet the water, with a small splash and the four men aboard, and the ropes being drawn back up to the ship.

"Men, have you forgotten a precious piece of cargo?" Archer called down to them. He waved me back and forth as if I were a piece of meat held over a lion's mouth. I almost blacked out completely as his fingers closed around my throat, but I managed to reach down with a back paw and bring my claws against his cheek, scrambling for a hold. It must have done the trick, for he gave a shout while the hand holding me jerked out and I was dropped, without much fanfare, over the side of the ship.

I wish I could report that I landed safely in the arms of my comrades in the longboat or, better, that I landed on all fours. But that is one myth I must dispel, as I did not land with any grace at all, and instead went face-first into the drink with my hindquarters following me at such an angle that I was completely flipped round. I heard the splash as I hit the water, then nothingness as the cold of the sea wrapped around me, seeping deep into my fur and biting at my skin. It was suddenly quiet as I'd never heard, and I opened my eyes beneath the surface in darkness, unsure even as to what way was up. I pedaled furiously with my paws, trying for any hold, and reached air, gasping and spewing seawater.

"Tibbs, Tibbs!" I heard my name being called, and suddenly a platform appeared beneath me, lifting me, water sploshing off around me. I immediately took to shivering and shaking as the oar that I clung to was pulled into the longboat. I looked up to see a large hand close over me and was shocked to find myself curled into the protective arms of Chippy. He had not been my biggest fan aboard, but he had just saved me from certain drowning without a second thought. In that moment he earned my loyalty.

A cheer and a roar went up from the ship, and I looked up to see all the sailors lined against the gunwale, watching, arms raised in triumph. It took me a moment to realize that they were cheering for *me*, and for Chippy for

saving me, and the chill from the sea left me momentarily, replaced by a warm feeling in my chest. I saw then that Archer had one hand on his pistol but the other on his cheek, covering the bloody scratches I had left behind. I've not made it a habit to take claws to my fellow sailors, but in some cases I've found it is necessary.

Archer held up his gun and turned to the sailors, ordering them back from the railing: "Go then, move on! I'll haze you! You'll join them if you aren't back to your posts!" he was yelling. But the men stood their ground, their faces now solemn as they watched our boat drift in the still water, away from the *Melissa Rae*.

There was no wind, and it felt as if we would sit looking up at the captain's great ship forever. But the sea works in mysterious ways, and there was, even in this stillness, a current that pulled us around the stern in a few moments' time, with the sailors aboard walking the deck slowly to keep us in eyeshot. A few removed hats and held them to their chests, but there were no tears, no calling out. And as she continued to drift away from us in the ocean, I saw the carefully painted letters that spelled *Melissa Rae* across her stern. The ship became no more than a brown-and-white shape as it floated out of sight.

"Men"—Moses leaned in with a whisper—"I've managed a bit of food and drink." He opened his greatcoat to reveal pockets stuffed with dried meat and hardtack biscuits and, perhaps most important, a large leather pouch of drinking water.

"How did you—" Sean started to ask.

"I slipped away, when the situation took a turn for the worse, and made quick to the galley."

Sean nodded his approval, and I could tell he respected the man's fast thinking. "Perhaps we can make do until another vessel passes, if we can stay on this route."

"He's right: there should be another by any day—we've not seen a ship for ages, and we know the paths they travel," Chippy added. "Your cleverness may have saved our hides," he said to Moses.

"And that's not all, gents." Moses grinned and reached out to put a hand on my back, but I found that even with the added warmth I could not stop the shivers that wracked my small, damp form. "I left that lot a little something from Jacob here as well."

Sean looked up at the man curiously. "From Jacob?"

"Aye," Moses went on, a glint in his eye. "Jacob's waste pan was in my galley, and I emptied it every day, over the side. But on this day I'd not had a moment—and Jacob here 'ad quite a go of it, didn't you, mate?" He ran his hand over my wet fur. It was an embarrassing truth—something I'd eaten, perhaps a bit of jerky tossed to me by one of the sailors, had not agreed with my guts. And my visits to the head—as we sailors call the toilet—were unpleasant, to say the least.

"Jacob's daily is now dumped, quite fully, into the flour bin and stirred in as much as I had time to accomplish. And there was even a bit left over for their drinking barrel."

Chippy roared with laughter, tipping his head back.

He looked to the ship as it slipped out of sight. "Good on you, Moses, and you too, Tibbs," he said with a smile. Then his eyes looked down at the form of the captain, lying still and in such calm repose that it seemed he wasn't even breathing, with his arms crossed over his chest.

Sean, though still smiling, also looked down and patted the captain's shoulder. "That's a story the man will appreciate, when he wakes."

"Aye," Chippy said quietly.

Sean took up an oar, as if suddenly realizing the seriousness of our situation. Chippy took the other oar, and without a word the two men began to row.

CHAPTER 17

CASTAWAYS

Our first night in the longboat was not entirely unpleasant, as the men were still in relatively good spirits, and around sunset the captain seemed to wake for a few moments.

"Am I at sea?" he asked, turning his head as Moses tried to pour a bit of drink into his throat. "Bring me my glass!" he coughed.

"Steady on, Captain, steady on," Moses murmured, resting the captain's head on a makeshift pillow of his own greatcoat wrapped around a coil of rope. I stood by his head and tried to knead the fabric into as soft a bedding as possible for the captain, purring at his ear.

The captain's eyes opened and he looked over at me, then up at the sky. Moses leaned to his ear and explained, in as concise terms as possible, our predicament, and what had become of his good ship, the *Melissa Rae*.

The captain seemed to take the news well. "Stay on the

trade route," he ordered, looking at Chippy. He reached carefully into the pocket of his trousers and came up with a gold circle attached to a chain. This he handed to Moses, who seemed to know just what to do with it. He pressed a small button on the top and the circle opened, a lid revealing a compass inside.

While I longed to bat the golden chain that dangled from the compass with my paws, I realized that this was not a time for play, and that I needed to focus on the issues at hand. Still, the glitter and shine that the compass threw off in the setting sunlight cast a moving sparkle on the inside of the boat, and I found myself chasing the reflected lights as they moved to and fro. The sailors seemed to take much pleasure in watching me race about the longboat. Moses tilted the golden compass to make the movements frantic, laughing with Chippy and Sean as I raced, my paws never able to catch them, until the sun moved so low as to not catch the metal of the compass any longer.

Moses shared his stores with us—pork and beef jerky and hardtack for the men, a bit of dried meat for me—and fed me water from the palm of his hand, and I curled up beside the captain, keeping my paws near his chest in the night to feel his reassuring breath moving in and out.

When I woke at dawn, Chippy and Sean were busily studying the sky and the information the compass held for them, trying to steer our boat in a direction that would put it in the path of an oncoming ship. Moses had shifted his greatcoat from under the captain, leaving him to rest on just a coil of rope for a pillow. At first, I wondered why he would take the man's only soft comfort, but I soon realized that Moses was pulling the coat apart and trying to build a makeshift sail of its pieces. Without needle or thread, this proved a taxing chore.

I arched my back and then stretched, moving from the captain's side to look overboard. The water was a dark, grayish blue in the dim light from the cloudy sky. I peered deep, trying to see anything within—a creature or even my own reflection. But it was boundless, with a dull surface, not sparkling and white-tipped like on a sunny, windy day. And then, all at once, I had a terrible feeling. I put my paws back down on the bottom of the longboat and looked to the sky, but the feeling did not leave me.

"Hungry, Jacob?" Moses grinned at me, tossing me a bit of dried pork. I eagerly picked up the meat with my teeth and set to gnawing it, hoping that perhaps he was right—the sick feeling in my stomach was just hunger. After eating, there was not much to do—no ship's hold to patrol for rats, no stove to curl up behind—and so I dozed in the humid heat, my head resting on my paws, and woke again to the sounds of Chippy and Sean fighting quite furiously, not with fists but with words.

"We've got to 'ave one man on watch at all times, but that man needs to know how to read a compass!" Chippy growled.

"And how is one to row and steer and keep the compass as well?" Sean asked.

"I'll have it now." Chippy grabbed at the golden compass

in Sean's hand, just as Sean yanked his hand back with it, and then a quiet plop was heard as the golden circle hit the water overboard. The two men glared at each other in silence, unable to believe what had just occurred—our only hope of finding our way home, now lost. I leapt to the side and looked over with my paws ready to reach, but the compass was too heavy—it had already sunk below.

"Ah, chaps, that had an engraving from the man's dead wife," Moses said softly. We all sat silently, as if in mourning, before Sean and Chippy were at each other again, arguing in the still heat and thick air.

"Mates!" Moses finally yelled. "There are but four men, and one beast, aboard this boat. We must do our best to keep peace." Chippy and Sean looked at him, scowling.

"And how do you propose we stay in the shipping lane now, with no compass?" Sean asked.

"When the stars are out, I know my way, as does the captain. We'll steer her right. By day, let the waves take us, and by night we'll find our way," Moses offered.

I lay beside the captain, my stomach rolling with the waves that lapped at the boat, and closed my eyes. I felt a drop on my back, but thought nothing of it—a stray wave or bit of splash. Then a second drop, and two more.

"What's this?" Moses looked up at the gray sky. "Rain, is it?"

Chippy quickly slipped off his boots and put them up on a bench in the boat. "Do the same, mates; we'll need the drink."

Sean took off his shoes and removed the captain's as

well, lining them up along the bottom of the boat to catch rainwater. Moses put his hat off his head and turned it upright. The sprinkles increased, making me thoroughly unhappy and damp, so I curled up beneath a bench as best I could, out of the angle of the driving rain.

"Some ship's cat we've got here," Chippy said harshly. "White paws and can't even warn of weather. Mrs. Tibbs would've been all over us with rain coming." He stripped off his shirt and held it over his head, hunching under it, blocking some of the drops.

Moses looked down at me, rain running off his bald head, and gave me a weak smile, but I could tell that even he was disappointed with how I had performed. I remembered my sick stomach of the morning, what I had thought was hunger, my queasy ache. It hadn't just been hunger—that had been the feeling! The warning that the weather was about to change—what I'd felt the first day aboard the *Melissa Rae,* before the storm that took my mother. I had known it but had not recognized the signs. I resolved then, as I curled into a tight ball in the damp bottom of the boat, that I would never again dismiss my intuition. It was my job to share this knowledge with the sailors, who did not possess my skills.

I drifted off to sleep as best I could in the gentle summer rain, and woke to darkness. Before I opened my eyes, I heard one of the men moaning, or snoring, a long low note. As I stretched and left Moses's side, I could tell that the air smelled clean and crisp, not heavy, as it had been since we'd left the *Melissa Rae.* The stars weren't quite out, but I could see, against the dark sky, puffy white clouds drifting by. A breeze! I felt it on my wet nose as I peeked over the edge of the boat. Finally the doldrums had lifted and we were in motion.

Then I heard again the sound that had woken me from my sleep—a deep, low moan. But when I looked around at the men, I saw that they were all soundly asleep. With no stars to study, they must have resigned themselves to shut-eye until the skies cleared. Even the captain seemed to be resting peacefully. Was the sound coming from the sea itself? It came again, rumbling up through the water, now a higher note at the end. I felt myself shaking. Who—or *what*—was below our boat? A light splash in the distance attracted my eyes, and I saw, faintly, something slick and black come up from the water, then slide back below the surface. It was shaped like a fish's tail but about the size of our whole boat . . . and looked like it was only a small part of whatever creature it was attached to.

I ran to Chippy—the largest and strongest man on our boat. He slept with his back to the stern, his shirt over him as a makeshift blanket. I hesitated. Should I wake him? Then the moan came again, shorter this time . . . but closer, too. I remembered how disappointed the men had been that I'd not warned them about the rain. I would never make that mistake again. I leapt onto Chippy's chest and startled him from sleep.

"What's this?" he yelled, swatting at me as he rolled over, curling into the angle of the stern. But I came back around, licking his nose and pawing his cheek beneath his eye patch. He brushed me away, as if I were a roach crawling over his face, but I saw his eye open a crack, so I let out a soft mew. "All right, then," he said, taking me into his arms and placing me on his chest. I kneaded his shirt, wanting him to fully wake, and then the sound did it for me: a long, low tone rippled up through the sea—it was unmistakable. I stood at attention, my ears perked, and held my breath.

But Chippy only let out a light laugh. "Your first time hearing a whale's song, Tibbs? They are mighty creatures but wouldn't take any notice of a little scrub like you. You've nothing to fear."

He ran his hand over my back and nestled down into the bottom of the boat, returning to sleep. But I continued to pace on his chest, worried over the sound. Whales? What type of creatures were these? How could a sea animal have such an enormous tail—why, it must be bigger than the *Melissa Rae* from end to end! The sound came again, followed by a splash, and I saw a large, dark shape with a stripe of white leave the water—not the whole of it, just a fraction—then roll back into the deep without a sound. The motion of its wake rocked the boat to and fro on gentle waves. I dug my claws into Chippy's shirt, and down into his skin, holding on tight for whatever might come next.

"Come on now, Tibbs," Chippy murmured, rolling over. "Let them sing you to sleep—the lullaby of the sea." He petted me gently then as I curled against him, trying to put the shape and size of the moaning sea monster out of my head. After a moment or two of silence, the big man whispered to me: "Whales used to put your mum out of sorts, too; she was never fond. Must be something that runs in the family."

With that I was content to return to sleep, in the crook of Chippy's strong arm. I was glad to hear that my mother had reacted in the same way to these moaning sea giants; they were obviously dangerous creatures, whether or not the sailors recognized that. I had done my job to wake and warn Chippy—if he chose to ignore my notice, so be it.

CHAPTER 18

MAN OVERBOARD

The days began to pass in a uniform fashion, just as they had aboard the *Melissa Rae*, but now with decidedly less food to eat and water to drink. The winds were good, from the west, and the weather fine. If we'd been aboard a vessel with sails, our travel would have been smooth. As it was, we were an angry, dirty lot in a longboat, trying to pass the time until we were rescued. During the sunny hours I could always find a place beside the captain to nap in warmth. At night I traveled around the boat, curling into the backs of knees where I could find them.

Once a day Moses would share his poached stores with us—half a stick of jerky for each man, the captain's ground into a fine paste that was fed to him with a bit of rainwater. The boots and hats were almost empty now, and the men looked to the clear and cloudless sky, wanting weather that would bring us more drink. My nose became dry and hard, and I saw the same effect on the men's lips, noses, and eyelids. Sean's lips beneath his bushy beard were white and cracked, and Moses's bald head had taken to peeling off flakes of skin in the baking sun.

The men tried their best to rest during the daylight hours, covered as well as they could be in their shirts and hats against the sun's rays. They needed their strength for the evening, to wake and watch the stars to chart our path and keep our little boat on the route of discovery—and the passage of other trade ships like the *Melissa Rae*. But none had yet come through. "A matter of time, boys, a matter of time," Chippy said.

During long spells of nothingness, Sean would put his head under his shirt and talk to someone—himself, I suppose—about the state of things. When he came out from under the shirt, he seemed himself again, so I did not question his antics, but I knew that Chippy and Moses found this behavior quite odd.

To entertain the men, sometimes Moses would flex the muscles of his arms and make the ladies who were tattooed there do a dance. I especially liked the drawing of the mermaid, as she was half lady and half fish, and when Moses made a fist just so, her tail seemed to move! I longed to dig my claws in to catch this flipping fin, but I knew it was the skin of my mate, so I held my sharps back and merely batted at her with a soft paw. I could have watched that beautiful mermaid dance forever. If Sean got into one of his dark moods, Moses would show him the dancing girls, and it never failed to make him laugh.

When the captain did awake, which was rarely, he

murmured to the men about the position of the night sky, what to look for, what to avoid, and how to steer our boat into the path of ships that we hoped would come soon. The sailors also knew the sky, and I trusted that they had put us on the right course. Maybe Chippy was right—it was just a waiting game.

I longed for the feeling of a storm in my gut, any sign that rain was coming, as I knew the sailors, my mates, needed more water to drink. Though the sea surrounded us, the water was not fit for man or beast, as I found when I lapped some up from the bottom of the boat. "Jacob, leave that!" Moses hollered at me. "The salt will make you sick, and you'll heave up what you do have in your belly." The water was so satisfying, I found his words hard to believe, but I obeyed. I took my small sips of water from Moses's hands, at midday, and tried to savor them.

The captain's health remained the same, though we were now more than seven days out. He looked hardy, his face lined and tan and his hair lightened from the relentless sun, but I knew that inside, his body was fighting a hard battle. At night he sometimes talked in his sleep, calling for someone named Catherine and giving orders to raise sails, swab decks. When he did this, I would curl up beside his ear and purr there, as this seemed to give him some measure of comfort.

I heard the men talk when the captain was not awake, debating his judgment, though they were loath to doubt him. Moses believed the stars should take us in another direction altogether, but they obeyed the captain, even in his febrile state, and steered our boat as he commanded.

What happened on the morning of the tenth day at sea I will recount here in as little detail as possible, as it is still a matter that brings me much sadness. It began when Chippy asked that Moses give them each their ration a bit early, as he felt he would not be able to rouse later to collect it. "My insides are eating themselves," he grumbled, taking the bit of meat from Moses. It was now just a quarter of a stick of jerky, and I noted that the men would chew this, bite after bite, and make it last for upward of an hour. Our hardtack biscuits had been exhausted three days prior.

Sean waved off the bit of meat, and I saw then, to my great surprise, that there were tears on his face. Then he started to cry, but not as I had seen men cry before. This was sobbing and sobbing, his messy head in his hands. He clawed at his own face, making red marks on his cheeks. I was so startled that I dove under the bench where Chippy was sitting. This was not the Sean that I knew.

"Here, man, have a bite of this." Moses tried again with the jerky, holding it out in his hand. But Sean shook his head. He wiped the back of his hand across his face and looked up at the men, suddenly smiling a huge, terrifying smile, his dry lips split and bleeding lines down into his teeth.

"I'm in the mind for fish, what of you lads?" he finally said. The men had tried, and failed, to catch any sea life, as they had neither bait nor hooks. And as Chippy had quickly pointed out, the types of fish that they could bring aboard were found only close to land. "Out here, 'tis whales and sharks and blues, others that we couldn't hope to wrestle onto the deck of this little boat," he explained. But just the talk of sea life made my mouth water with the idea of salty fish-head soup, and I felt as if I would give my own tail for just one bite.

Before any of the men could react, Sean had stripped off his shirt, revealing his badly burned shoulders beneath, and removed his boots and trousers, leaving nothing but his underdrawers intact. I could tell from the sparkle in his eye that he was deadly serious about the task at hand, but something seemed off. Even his voice was not that of the Sean I had come to know.

"You're not well," Moses said calmly, moving to sit beside Sean in the boat. "Let's have a talk about it." He put his arm around Sean's shoulders, but Sean quickly brushed him off, his face taking on a sour look.

"You have a nerve to tell me how I'm feeling," Sean spat out, his face mean, growling. "Hiding meats from the rest of us. I've heard your teeth at night—how much do you have hidden away in there?" He pulled at Moses's shirt, tearing it open, until Chippy moved forward and grabbed his arm, rocking the boat hard enough to nearly upset us all.

"Sean, think on your words!" Chippy barked.

"This one's hiding meat—he's eating it at night, undercover, and not sharing it with us!" As Sean spoke, his voice was high, sounding almost like Melissa's. "He has butter! And biscuits! Molasses!"

"It's not true," Moses said quickly, raising his hands. "You've seen all I brought aboard. I've no interest in cheating anyone or hiding anything. You must believe me."

"I'll 'ave a look into your greatcoat," Chippy warned him, moving to the stern to take up Moses's torn and ratty coat. He had tried to figure a sail with it but had finally given up, leaving the coat as a blanket and sun cover, the pockets storage for our rations.

Moses nodded, watching as Chippy searched the pockets. He came out with two half sticks of jerky and some crumbs of biscuit, along with the leather pouch that contained the end of our water. As the crumbs tumbled to the wooden bottom of the boat, I raced over and put them on my tongue, though they were too small even to taste. "All is as it should be—look, Sean," Chippy implored, showing the pockets turned out. "You've gone right mad from the sun and need a rest, some drink."

But Sean was not satisfied with Chippy's reveal, nor Moses's claims of innocence. In one swift motion he pulled away from the men and was over the side of the boat, splashing into the water. "I'll catch us a fish!" he yelled back at the men, swimming out from the boat. "That's it! That's the way!"

I put my paws up to the side of the still-rocking boat and looked out at Sean as he swam toward the horizon in clean strokes. I meowed for him, calling him back. Moses and Chippy also took up calling him: "Sean! Sean! Come on, man. Let's have a drink and a talk; it's not as bad as all that!"

"Your siren is waiting here!" Moses called over the side, pointing to the mermaid on his arm as Sean's form grew smaller in the water. "All is not lost, come! Turn about! I'll make the girls dance a special jig, for you alone!"

Sean stopped for a moment and looked back at the men as if he was confused as to who they even were, or how they knew his name. His hair and beard were wet, but he was too far out for me to see his eyes, to know what might have been going through his mind. Moses took in a deep breath, hoping for the best, but it was not to be. Sean returned to his swimming, off into the distance, as the men called after him.

After a moment Moses stopped calling Sean's name and picked up the oars, ready to row. He had gone only a few paces before Chippy grabbed his arm, shaking his head. "He's gone altogether; don't you add to it," he said gruffly.

Moses paused, looking out at his friend in the waves, then dropped the oars, putting his head into his hands. As we watched, Sean's form moved out toward the horizon, becoming just a head above the waves, then a spot, then nothing. As evening fell, not one among us uttered a sound, looking out to the place where we had last seen our friend, watching the waves as if he might return.

Death at sea is a strange thing, a sudden thing. A ship on the waves is not a proper place for mourning, though Moses and Chippy did engage in a prayer over clasped hands before turning in for some shut-eye. They would be awake again in the pitch-black, well before dawn, to study the stars and steer our vessel. "There, but for the grace of God, we will follow," Moses said quietly as he curled into himself on one end of the boat.

The leather pouch that held our water was almost empty. And with two half sticks of jerky left, it did seem as though perhaps Sean had the right idea. End with dignity, with waves crashing over your head, or end as a pile of bones in the bottom of this longboat, food for gulls—those were the choices before us.

That night, a restless sleep came only after a long battle. I could not find comfort in my usual spots by the captain's side nor behind my mates' knees. I woke looking for Sean, thinking that perhaps the events of the day had not been real. But as I counted the dark shapes curled in our boat, it was clear that our number was now reduced from four men to only three. My dreams were full up with visions of my mother and Sean, under the waves, struggling to get up, sea creatures, big as I'd ever seen, chasing them down. When I woke in the dark, it was to thoughts of Sean, his bushy red beard, how he'd put me into his greatcoat pocket on that loading-to day, showing me such kindness—how far away that all seemed now! I longed for the cool, dark hold of the *Melissa Rae*, the smell of gunpowder. My soft calico cloth behind the stove, now lost forever.

Sleep would not return, and so I looked over the side, to the moonlit water around us. I stared hard into the horizon, wondering if a miracle might occur and I would see Sean's red hair bobbing on the waves, coming back to us. But it was not to be. I padded over to the other side of the boat, pausing on the captain's chest to be sure of his steady breath.

As I looked out over the sea, I saw, in the distance, white waves cresting and falling. Cresting and falling. I watched their rhythm for a moment or two, soothed by the simple ebb and flow, before a ripple of shock traveled up my paws and down my spine. Waves, cresting white! That meant one thing: they were striking something. There was something out there!

I leapt over the captain's sleeping form and jumped onto Moses's back. I tried to meow at his ear, but found that my sun-parched throat could make nothing more than a tiny mew. So I scratched, lightly, my paws moving down his back. He murmured something and made to roll over on me, so I jumped down and hurried to the other side of the longboat, where Chippy was asleep with his mouth hanging open, his arms at his sides. I crawled up his chest and put my nose to his face, licking him roughly.

"Get off!" He brushed me away with one motion. "I told you, cat, it's just the whales!"

I returned to Moses now, full of urgency. The men needed to see what I had seen, before it was too late. I crawled up Moses's sleeping form, clawing as I went.

"I've a mind to put you overboard!" Moses finally yelled, sitting up. I mewed, as best I could with a dry mouth, and stood at attention at starboard, showing him what I had seen. Moses rubbed the sleep from his eyes and looked out over the sea. He blinked once, twice, then rubbed his eyes again. "My heavens, Chip! Wake and have a look!"

Chippy grumbled and sat up a bit, licking his lips. "What's the bother?"

Now, as I watched, something new appeared: a shadow loomed in the moonlight, just beyond the white-crested breakers, a big, dark mound rising out of the water.

"It's not a bother; it's land. Land ho! Land ho! And Jacob here has found it!"

CHAPTER 19

THE ISLAND

It took only a little effort on the part of the two able-bodied men aboard to bring our little vessel onto the beach of the island; the tide and waves had strength of their own and pulled us into a safe and cozy cove in the early-morning hours.

"Captain, wake and have a look!" Moses whispered into his ear as the island loomed over us. It was like one big green hill, surrounded at the bottom by black rocks, the shape of the hill soft and rounded, like a cat arching his back.

"Aye." The captain opened his eye just a squint. "I knew there were islands near here. You've done it, lads."

I now understood why the captain had been steering us this way, to the doubts of even Moses—perhaps he knew that a trade vessel would not be along, and had directed us to the islands instead. It didn't matter now—we were saved!

Our longboat dashed through the breakers that surrounded the island, taking each with higher and higher lifts, crashing down in the sea spray, until at last we were plopped down in the gentle waves of a still and quiet cove of bright green water, just beyond the reef. The men used oars and pushed us into land, Chippy jumping out as soon as the boat was near enough to pull us in.

Moses, too, leapt from the boat, balancing carefully on his peg, and put his face down to the black rocks of the shore, which seemed to come straight up from under the ocean waves. The men laughed and hugged each other, dancing a jig as best they could on the uneven ground. I put my paws over the edge of the stern and tried to climb out.

"Here you are, mate." Moses grabbed me under my middle and plopped me down onto the small rocks. He and Chippy turned to the captain, lifting him carefully out of the boat.

I tried to walk but found that the rocks moved beneath my paws in a most unusual way, shifting from under me as if they were more water. I wobbled and tumbled forward, face-first. At least the rocks here were smooth and battered by the sea, not rough and jagged like those under our boat as we came into the island.

"Our wee kitty has no land legs!" Moses laughed, looking over at me as he and Chippy carefully placed the captain down.

"A rocky shore as this can take some getting used to," Chippy agreed, slipping off his boots and putting his bare feet down on the black rocks. "But I could certainly get used to it!"

"Aye." Moses smiled. He picked me up, saving me from falling again, and put me over his thin shoulder. "Come with me, lad, and we'll have a look for some flat earth and water to drink."

"I'll stay with the good captain," Chippy agreed, "and pull up the boat." He went down to the water and tugged our longboat higher onto the shore, securing it with a rope and a nearby rock.

Moses turned toward the greenery that bordered the cove, and took me with him. I looked out over his shoulder at the surroundings. I had never been on land—born on a boat and always on one—until this point in my life, so I knew little of the things around me. As Moses moved farther from the black rocks of the beach and into the thick foliage that bordered it, green leaves brushed my face, and I batted at them with my paws, unsure if they were friend or foe. As the morning sun began to rise, it lit up the plants and short trees of the island. I'd never seen such colors—stalks of bright green, flowers and leaves of every variety, reds and yellows flashed by. The smells were divine: the scent of the fresh sea air mingled with the sweet pollen of the petals around us.

"Ah, it's heaven, it is, Mr. Tibbs." Moses ran a hand over my back and headed straight inland, as if he knew right where his destination was. "With a hill of this size, there should be water nearby, funneled down from up high."

Moses tromped through the vegetation as it grew thicker; the plants became small tree trunks and then vines. He took out his knife and cut away at some of the large palm leaves and stringy vines that blocked our path. "We're getting close; I can feel it in me bones," he murmured, more to himself than to me. I held on tightly with my paws, putting my claws into his shirt. I was still unsure of this new place called "land," and I didn't quite want to be put down yet. Besides, from the vantage point of Moses's shoulder, I could see everything to my liking.

Moses cut away at a thick vine, then stopped in his tracks for a moment. He knelt down to the ground and put his fingers out to touch a small reddish-green plant. I slid down from his shoulder and put my paws to the ground, which was very different from the rocks of the shore, more solid and covered with soft leaves. I preferred it.

I paced for a moment, sniffing at the strange things around me, while Moses inspected his plant. I tipped my nose up at the air, filled with scents I didn't recognize. I couldn't tell if they were animal or vegetable, but none of them were unpleasant. Moses picked a few leaves of the plant and tucked them into his shirt pocket. "Come, lad." He called me with a quick whistle, and started back into the greenery. I followed close at his boot heels, wishing to be picked up again. It wasn't long before the ground beneath my feet began to feel sticky, then wet. I meowed to Moses to slow down as my paws came up muddy, but he kept moving forward, more urgently now, leaving me in his wake as he pushed through big green fern leaves.

"There she is! Just as I thought!" Moses pushed aside a palm leaf and crouched down to me. "A sight for sore eyes." In front of us loomed the big green hill that we had seen from the boat, only now it did not look quite so soft and round but was surrounded by jagged black rocks that led up onto a thickly covered steep mountain. Down one side a flow of water tumbled—not much, but to sailors who had been without fresh water for so many days, it looked like a river from heaven!

Moses raced ahead to the small stream that lay at our feet. He knelt down and put his face into the water; I followed him, lapping up the cold, clean stream. The water tasted so wonderful, not like the inside of a leather boot or an old hat, so fresh and crisp. It was the best water I'd had in my young life. We both drank, silently, for a long time before Moses spoke. "The nectar of the gods, that—better than a bottle of rum from the islands!" He pulled his leather bag from over his shoulder and rinsed it in the water before filling it to overflowing.

"Now let's take this back to the captain and to Chippy." He patted his shoulder, and I leapt up, pushing my whiskers against his face and purring my pleasure at having a wet nose yet again. When we returned to the shore, the sun was over the island, and I expected it would be eight bells on the ship. Chippy had carried the captain to the greenery, off the rocks, and propped him sitting up on a pile of clothes—Moses's greatcoat and, I saw with great sadness, Sean's old shirt and trousers.

Moses tossed Chippy the leather pouch filled with water, and the man caught it with a bigger grin than I'd ever seen on his face. He snapped the lid and drank deeply before turning to the captain to rouse him. "Sir, a bit of the drink for you—as fresh as you're likely to find." He held the pouch to the captain's mouth and helped him to take it in.

The fresh water seemed to do the captain worlds of good, as did being on solid land. Later in the day he opened his eyes and really seemed to take in his surroundings. It was then that he noted the absence of a crew member, and he asked after Sean, only to be told the terrible truth. He quickly closed his eyes and returned to his fitful sleep, as if unable to face the reality.

Before the heat of the day could bear down on us, the men found a series of sticks in the green area and used those to prop up the longboat overturned, and so we had a makeshift shelter, or at the very least a bit of shade over our heads. Moses collected some of the larger palm leaves and put them down as a mat over the ground to soften our floor, but I still found that I could feel the bumps beneath me when I tried to lie down for a nap next to the captain.

Moses and Chippy hunted for food and were terribly pleased to find a greenish-blue shelled creature living under the larger rocks of the beach. Chippy heaved over a rock, and Moses jabbed at the creature with a spear he had fashioned, which was just a long stick with his small pocketknife secured to one end. When they had a collection of the small monsters, which looked more like big spiders than food to me, they lit a beach fire with their flint rock and some dried plants. Then they roasted the creatures on long sticks until their shells turned bright red, and cracked them open as if they were nuts and ate the meat inside.

I've learned since that this shelled creature is quite a delicacy—one that I've been served only a number of times since our days on the island. To be completely honest, I didn't have much taste for it then, nor do I now—the meat has a rubbery texture and lack of flavor that I find unappealing. I far prefer fish of any kind—even a few days old. But, at the time, with food scarce and my growing body demanding more, I ate what was given to me and savored every bite. I also took great pleasure in joining my mates for hunting the shelled creatures, chasing them across the rocky beach if they escaped Moses's crafted spear. They had an odd way of moving quickly that followed no reason as they skittered to the side across the rocks. Yet they could leap with great speed and snapped viciously with their large front claws when I came near.

By our first afternoon on the island, we had captured a whole pile of the shelled creatures. And by evening, we had eaten so many of them and drunk so much water, I thought my stomach might burst. I lay by the captain for a quick nap, but Moses had other plans.

"I believe I've seen this herb before," he told Chippy,

pulling the reddish leaves from his pocket. He ripped one of the leaves in half and smelled it. "Looks a bit different, but I'd barter it's the same as what I've seen on the Verde Islands."

Chippy was still finishing up his crab feast, licking his fingers and drinking from the leather pouch. "What of it?" he growled, obviously uninterested.

"Used to make a medicine, from what I remember. Those are long-ago times for me, but if I'm right . . ." He looked over at the captain, who now lay with his eyes closed again, his face pale and waxy.

"Worth a try, mate," Chippy said quietly. "But I'll be right surprised if a leaf can make him well again."

Moses went down to the waves, and I followed along behind him, watching as he scooped up a handful of seawater. While the sun set spectacularly over the island, casting a red glow over everything, he pounded the leaves between two black rocks with a splash of water. When he was done, we went back up to the fire, me scrabbling over the black rocks just like one of the green crabs. Moses put the mixture on a rock near the fire and let it heat until it was a warm paste. Then, in the last crimson light of the day, he unwrapped the captain's leg—the dressing for which had not been changed during our time in the longboat.

I heard Moses pull in a breath through gritted teeth, and I came around him, rubbing my fur along his side. The sight of the captain's leg was a horrible thing—from the knee down, it was black with a large, ugly wound.

Moses looked down at the tincture he had created for the captain's festering leg, and I saw his face tighten. I sniffed at the stuff on the rock, then looked up at him. I meowed to snap him from his thoughts, which I knew were dark. "Let's give it a go then, shall we?" he said quietly. I watched him spread the warm paste over the worst of the captain's wound, also moving up and around the entire leg.

The captain opened his eyes but did not look to be in pain. I moved to his side so he could pet me and rubbed against him, purring, hoping to distract him from looking down at what had become of his once-strong body.

"I've seen this used before, when I traveled under another captain," Moses explained. My mind went to the memory of a night in the galley, the men talking about a cruel ship Moses had worked on. Was it there that he learned the magic of these herbs and leaves? "It may do you some good."

"You have my thanks, Mr. Moses," the captain said, his voice dry. "My deepest thanks. I fear that this"—he stopped and motioned around him at the island—"all of this is my doing, and for that I am gravely sorry."

"Heal, Captain, and all will be well."

The captain's eyes were watery. "And what of Sean, and the souls still aboard the *Melissa Rae*? It cannot be worth one man's life to lose so many others." He closed his eyes again and let out a sigh as Moses rewrapped his leg in a piece of cloth torn from his own greatcoat.

"When you have done right, Providence smiles upon

you," Moses said quietly. "And when you have done wrong, woe unto you." He laid two hands over the wrapped wound and turned his head up to the stars, as if throwing a wish into the sky.

That first night I curled in beside the captain, but he did not stir. The sound of the waves kept me awake, as they crashed loudly on the shore, over and over again. And when the water pulled back into the sea, it took rocks with it, which rumbled over each other and created a terrible racket. I saw, in the darkness, things moving down on the beach, small creatures making their way to and fro across the rocks. I was not used to being around other creatures—save for rats—and I did not care for the mysterious shadows. But when I closed my eyes, a vision was there, of the captain's leg and the dark hollow spot, so I kept my eyes open. If he was lost to us now, all of this—being put out in the longboat, Sean's death, our near starvation—would be for naught. So, as Moses said, he would have to live, and be well.

CHAPTER 20

LIFE ON LAND

Perhaps it was the fresh water and island fruits, or the roasted crab, but by the middle of the next day, the captain looked somewhat better. His eyes took on a brightness that had been absent for weeks. He stayed awake for more than an hour and made conversation with the men. I sat next to him, my paws out in front of me, eyes closed, just soaking in the island sun and listening to their talk until I felt confident he was in good hands. Then I stretched, arched my back, and, after receiving a quick scratch behind the ears from Moses, went off to explore the island.

At first I was careful to follow the same path that Moses and I had taken into the greenery the day previous—our steps were still laid flat, for the most part. And as I went, I could hear the voices of the men close behind me. But now I could inspect everything with thorough care, as I had not had the time to do yesterday. One shiny green plant that grew close to the ground had spikes like pointy teeth coming out of its leaves—I discovered this too late, as I was poked in the nose by a needle. I wanted very much to claw it to bits, but I held my temper, as I was sure I could do without the needles lodged in my paws and fur.

I slowly made my way to the stream, finding odd beetles and insects of all sorts along the way. Some were quite large—the beetles with hard, brightly colored shells were almost the size of my paw. When I tried to play with them, they opened their backs into two wings and lazily flew off, up high into the plants. Most of the plants on the island could not support my weight; their stalks were green and not strong enough. But a few, the trees that bore fruit, were easy to climb when I dug my nails into their bark—they were just like the masts on the *Melissa Rae*.

Whenever I thought of the ship, my stomach took on a queasy feeling, and I tried to quickly banish the memory. Still, picturing my calico bed, the last thing of my mother's that I had, now stuffed behind the stove on a ship that was far from me, made my heart ache. I climbed up one small tree and held on to a branch at a height where I could see out over the ocean, to the breakers that crested white on the rocky reef beyond our beach. I watched for a long time, perhaps hoping to see Sean's red hair rise above the waves. I told myself not to hope, but there was a little part of me that thought there was a chance he had survived, perhaps washed up on an island like this one. I wanted to imagine it could be so. I also kept my eyes open for ships, as the men had said there was possibility of that as well.

After taking a long drink from the cold stream, I heard a welcome sound: the captain's whistle. He was calling for me! I returned to the beach and to my mates, who had kept themselves very busy at different tasks. Chippy was cooking a thick paste, made from the white, sticky juice of the palm plants, over the fire. This "glue" would be used in repairing any small holes in our longboat. The captain was still in the same spot but was now sitting up and picking oakum from our small stretch of rope, perhaps for the same repairs.

"There's our young man!" he said when he saw me. I noted that he and Chippy had bathed and both removed the bushy hair from their faces, though why, I do not know, as I found it suited them nicely.

I looked about for Moses and saw his small, stooped form down at the rocks, hunting for crab. I joined him there and at once realized that I had been wrong: he was not looking for crabs—he was fishing! He had fashioned a trap by tying a bit of crabmeat to a string for bait and stood out on a large black rock, dangling it into the water below.

"Shush you, Jacob, not a sound," he whispered to me. "Don't scare off our lunch." I stood back in the shadow of his legs and watched as small, silvery fish circled the bait. If they had not been under the water, I would've leapt on them in a wink! Their sparkle in the sunlight and quick movements drove me mad, and I soon found myself pacing the rock, my mouth watering at the sight.

"Jacob, go on now." Moses pushed at me with his foot.

"No fish will come to bait with a creature such as you looming over them!"

I reluctantly went back to the beach, taking my time to inspect overturned rocks and smelling the crabs that had recently been there. Just as I was about to catch a sea beetle in my claws, Moses yelled out. I looked over to see him holding his makeshift rod up over his head, a good-sized silver fish hanging from it.

The captain and Chippy hollered from the beach. "Good on you, mate!" Chippy said. I raced out to the rock to escort Moses and his catch back to land, wanting to take some credit for his good luck. I had, in fact, gone away as he had asked, and that must have been what brought the fish.

I peered down over the rocks to look for more fish, and my reflection in the water below startled me: Was that my mother? No—it was me, and yet I was her spit and image. I was growing, and taking on the shape of a real cat now, not a kitten. When I put my face down to the water, I saw her reflection looking back at me, the same high *M* in the fur on my forehead, the same white whiskers and green eyes. Aside from my white paws, I was a miniature of her.

Moses quickly cut and gutted the fish, roasting it over the fire on a stick. He tossed me some bits from the fish's belly, which I found most delicious. Why the men chose not to eat these parts, I will never know, but they pleased me more than their precious shelled creatures, and I ate them quickly off the rocks and meowed for more. "You'll have more, Tibbs, if you stop that racket!" Chippy barked at me, taking a hunk of now-white cooked fish meat from Moses and stuffing it into his mouth.

"If I can smoke a stack of these before the winds change, we should be right set," Moses said to the captain, handing him a piece of the fish.

"Aye," the captain agreed. "Those breakers will be the devil to cross unless the wind is with us. And even then . . ." He glanced over at Chippy.

The big man looked out over the ocean, which was beautiful and blue. "I think she can weather it, Captain. With sails and three men to weigh her down."

"And one cat," Moses added with a wink.

"Yes, what of this lazy oaf?" Chippy scooped me up and rolled me over in his hands. "What's this, a belly on our skinny little runt?" He ran his hand roughly over my stomach, now full with fish, and I purred, trying to catch his fingers with my paws. "He's grown fat and sassy!" Chippy rarely showed me any affection, so to be tousled by him meant the men were in good spirits indeed!

It soon became clear to me that, while we were living well and happy on our island, the men still longed for Liverpool, for home, and planned to fashion their small ship into a proper sailing vessel. As the men continued to talk, I understood that they were waiting now not only for the captain to be well again, but for the winds to change, as without the wind at our backs, the breakers that protected our pretty reef would also keep us trapped here on this island.

While awaiting the winds—which could take days, or

weeks, to change direction—the men busied themselves. Chippy set to building a mast from a long, thin tree trunk. Moses had managed to create a sewing needle from one of the spikes on the vicious plant I'd encountered in the greenery. The men worked the afternoon away, Moses sewing as he sat with his fishing rod out on the far rock, a makeshift hat of palm leaves atop his burned-brown head. And Chippy used the small knife to cut branches from the tree trunk, making the mast smooth and strong.

As they worked, the men told yarns and talked of their loved ones at home—their wives, especially, who were both described in such a way that made me believe they were very lovely indeed. The captain rarely spoke of his deceased wife, who I understood had passed away from a terrible sickness, but he did mention Melissa, and sent up an occasional prayer that her health was holding, and that the summer months in Liverpool would restore her. To be a sailor meant spending long spells away from loved ones—this I learned early on—and my duty as a ship's cat was to bring comfort to my mates when they grew lonely or ached for home.

In the evening Moses again changed the captain's dressing on his leg, and lo! What a wondrous miracle had occurred there—the leg was turning from purple to red in some parts, and Moses decreed that this was good. "It's healing, Captain; the poison is going. 'Ave a look," he implored, but the captain would not look down.

"Do what you must, Mr. Moses, but do not ask me to look upon the waste I've wrought," he said sadly, then returned to his task of braiding vines into a thick, strong rope.

That night we ate several fish, and Moses set some to smoking over the fire when it got low. These we could take aboard our newly fashioned vessel and have as food for the journey home to Liverpool, along with some fruits that Moses was drying, spread on leaves out on the rocks where they could gather sun.

I cozied in against my mates by the fire as they laughed and sang songs after the sun had set. It felt much like being in the galley on the *Melissa Rae*, with the captain well again. Chippy told a terrifying yarn about a ghost ship that arrived in port with only one body aboard: a skeleton still dressed in captain's clothes, tied to the wheel, clutching a silver cross. All other bodies had been lost, who knows where, at sea. "Dead men tell no tales," Chippy said in a deep growl, his dark eye patch a black shadow in the night. A shiver went down my back at the details, and I tried not to listen as the men told stories of other voyages gone wrong, of strange events at sea.

I looked out over the ocean, at the breakers cresting white in the moonlight—that was my true home and always would be. The island life was a good one, but it was not for me, and I longed to be back on the waves, guiding my captain and his sailors homeward.

CHAPTER 21

SKELETON CREW

As soon as our survival on the island seemed assured, and the days passed in an orderly fashion, the men began to talk of revenge. They all worked hard, even the captain, setting our vessel to right and stockpiling supplies and food for the journey home. The captain sat in the morning sun, braiding vines into thick rope, for what I did not know, but with his experience at sea, I was sure it would serve some purpose. On one such morning that dawned clear and bright, the talk was decidedly dark.

"If we dock in Liverpool before they've a chance to return from New York Harbor, we'll have our day before the judge," Moses exclaimed.

But the captain shook his head sadly. "It was within rights, what Archer did. Though it pains me to speak it, I'm afraid I have no standing—I fear I've lost the *Melissa Rae* and, along with her, my crew and life's income as well."

"The ship is owned by Archer and his father, so they've the right to do what they please; there's no way around that, to be sure," Chippy agreed with him. "But I've my own form of justice, which will be administered swiftly when I lay eyes on that yellow-bellied fool," he grumbled, holding up both fists in a boxer's stance.

"Aye, I think you've given him a taste of that before!" Moses joked, and I remembered the storm, when Chippy had almost slapped Archer across the face. I didn't much like to remember that night, so I moved away from the men and their angry talk, toward the edge of the trees. The men were working so hard, I felt somewhat useless and underfoot. There was no ship's hold for me to patrol, no rats for me to catch. I was not, on the island, earning my keep in any way—and I was eating a good portion of the men's fish while at my leisure!

As I sniffed along the edge of the rocky coast, I remembered Chippy rubbing my tummy, noting that I'd gone a bit soft around the middle. He was right; I had become "fat and sassy," as he'd said. I nosed my way under the low leaves of a plant and a thought came to me. The greenery of the island grew quite thick, and the men had to cut their path through, even to gather more vines near the stream. But for me, traversing the place was easy, as I could slink low, below the thick foliage, and walk stealthily in the cool shade close to the ground. I decided to go into the woods past the stream, to have a look about and see what I could bring back for the men. Moses had been having a hard time locating enough of the reddish-green plant to make the medicine for the captain's leg—perhaps I could discover a bit of it and lead one of the men there? I had to try, as lying in the sun across a warm rock on my round belly was hardly respectable for a sea cat. What would my mother make of my current laziness and lack of duty?

I passed the stream, stepping gingerly over the water on small rocks, balancing carefully, and stopped to have a quick drink on the other side. This was my first time crossing over the stream, as usually my daily journeys stopped once I'd reached water. Here the plants and vegetation grew thick and tangled, almost down to the ground, and getting beneath them was a task even for me. As I slunk low and crawled along, I kept my eyes open for the small red-and-green leaves that Moses would want. I found that the beetles had discovered the place before me and populated the base of several plants, families of all sizes, bobbing about and doing whatever was their work. I stopped to watch a few larger ones making their way and batted at them with my paw, but they seemed uninterested in me, slowly returning along their plodding way, and so I left them be.

After a few more paces, all at once sunlight shone through, and I found myself coming into a small clearing. Here the ground looked as though it had been tidied. A charred black spot surrounded by rocks smelled as if a fire had been there, long ago. Grasses and some smaller plants filled the space, but not the taller plants I had just traversed, and no vines crossed. I had a clear view of the

sky. I nosed around the perimeter a bit, looking for clues, then went to lie, just for a moment's rest, in a sunny spot dead center.

There was a pile of little white sticks on the ground, and when I moved them with my paw I saw that they were attached to a longer white stick. And that stick was oddly attached to more pieces of white, larger now, one a round ball shape. I batted at the ball and it rolled over in the short grass, revealing dark circles upon the other side and . . . teeth! I leapt back, horrified to realize I was looking at a human being, much like my mates, only with his skin off! The white sticks were bones, skeleton bones. I stared, shivering and thinking only of Chippy's horrible story. Was this a ghost, a sailor lost at sea? I moved carefully toward the skull and pawed it again. It rolled over, the white teeth smiling up at me in an endless grimace.

As I nosed around the bones, I caught no scent of man, only of the outdoors and plants. But when I reached his other side, I noted, with a sickening dread, that there was some bit of rope attached to him, where his arms would once have been. It looked as though his hands had been bound, as if the rope, though now quite disintegrated, had been tied many times.

A stick snapped somewhere behind me, and I spun around, claws out and ready to fight. I scanned the dark, shadowy woods for movement and prowled low. We had assumed we were alone on the island, but perhaps that was not the case. I growled to let my watcher know that I, too, was watching. But no one stepped from the woods, and there was no sound except those I made. I backed away from the clearing, leaving the bones and ropes where they were. As soon as I was under the shadowy cover of the plants and trees, I turned and ran as fast as my paws could carry me, leaping over the stream when I reached it. I had no time to search for Moses's plants, instead racing back to the men on the beach.

When I collapsed, panting, at Moses's feet, he took little notice of me, continuing to play some kind of tile game that Chippy had carved from shells. I looked around our small shelter and realized that the captain was missing—he was not in his usual spot. I leapt to my feet and set to crying, nosing his makeshift pillow and taking in his scent. He could not go into the woods alone! What if he were to end up like that pile of bones I had seen? I could not bear it!

"Stop that racket! Your master's down to the sea; he's having a soak," Chippy growled, motioning toward the cove as he turned over a white tile.

I raced to the black rocks and found the captain, without a stitch of clothing on, sitting in a small pool of seawater. Chippy and Moses must have carried him all this way, as he could not yet stand on his own. His bandage was off, and his leg looked fine indeed, much changed, the color almost back to normal again. He scrubbed his skin with a bit of cloth and looked up at me, his eyes bright and sparkling. "Mr. Jacob Tibbs, it's a fine day for island life, is it not? We will sail as soon as this wind changes—are you ready to set to?" He reached up with a wet hand and petted my head. Though I didn't care for the drops of water, his hand was always welcome on my back, and I purred my approval of the plan.

"Soon we will be home again, with Melissa and safe as houses, with a proper tub for baths. Though I may miss this paradise. I've grown quite fond of it." He looked back over his shoulder at the green gem of an island.

When I think back to the island and our time there, what I remember most is the clear, cool water that tumbled down from the green mountain, and how well the men grew while drinking from it. How the captain's leg healed, after weeks of festering and infection. And how, once we left the island, our fortunes changed so quickly.

CHAPTER 22

SUN AND SEA

How many weeks of fair weather passed while we lived on the island, I've no way of knowing. Moses kept marks on a gray rock, leaving a line for each day, but I took little notice of how many accumulated there. Instead, I busied myself helping my mates capture crabs, fish, and generally remain merry, which, on the beautiful green-cloaked island, was easy to do. Then one morning we woke with gray clouds hanging low, but surprisingly, this change in the weather meant good fortune for us as sailors. Captain Natick took a nearby palm leaf and secured it to a twig like a flag, then stuck it into the rocks.

"The wind is with us," he declared, watching the green leaf blow in the breeze. "We'll need every lick of it to get over those breakers."

Moses was wrapping dried fish in palm fronds and securing them into bundles at the bottom of our boat. "And what if it's not enough, Captain?"

"Then we'll be dashed on the rocks," Chippy mumbled in his gruff voice as he rigged our makeshift sail to its mast. He lifted his eye patch and rubbed the closed lid beneath. "But try we must, eh, Captain?"

The captain motioned for Chippy to help him stand. Moses had carved him a sturdy crutch from a large branch, and once he was pulled up, he could lean upon it. "I've a way that may work, but we'll need both of you and that sail on the wind to do it." He looked with a wary face at the wooden mast and the sail that Moses had sewn, now lying in the bottom of our boat.

I finished up the breakfast that Moses had tossed me—a last meal of crabmeat, roasted over the open fire—then drank water from my bowl, which was really just an overturned seashell. I paced the rocky shoreline, back and forth, looking out over the waves, waiting for a sign, but none came. I had no ill feeling in my gut, no twitching of my whiskers. The sky was gray and the wind had changed course, but there was no storm to be seen or felt, at least not a great enough one to worry us.

When the men were ready, they doused the fire with seawater, and Moses and Chippy carried the boat down to the water's edge. Moses lifted me gently and placed me inside on a bench; then both men helped the captain aboard before climbing in. No one spoke as the men rowed us out from the island. I looked from face to face but saw only tension and scowls. I would soon learn why.

As we neared the place in the ocean where our quiet, calm cove turned into a reef of black rock and white-crested waves, the captain spoke: "Here's where, men; this is the place"—and at those words Moses and Chippy dashed their oars and jumped into the water! They each held a side of the boat and put their boots down on the black rocks, jagged and sharp. How Moses was able to secure himself on his peg, I've no idea The waves became larger here, lifting the bow of the boat and tipping it almost upright with each roll. I found myself tossed and tumbled, scratching along the length of the boat as I tried to find footing with my paws. The men held the boat steady and paced themselves with beats to time the passage of the waves, waiting until just the right moment to push her forward. Then they both leapt, soaked to the bones, back into the boat, grabbed the oars, and rowed furiously.

At the next set of breakers, I had no idea how we would get over the crest of the waves—some looked to be over twenty feet high. The captain held fast to the side, his knuckles white, and I scooted between his feet, my claws digging into the bottom of the wooden longboat. The front of the boat rode up, up, and finally over the wave just before the set of breakers.

"Now!" the captain yelled over the sound of the crashing waves. Moses handed his oars to the captain and leapt over the side again, his head going under for a moment. Chippy was already over the other side and holding to as the biggest wave I'd seen yet came to bear down on us. The captain reached forward and pulled a rope from the bottom of the boat, yanking it to him—with it, up came the mast and sail that Moses and Chippy had rigged. As the sail came up, the fabric quickly filled with air, thrusting us forward. The men pushed off the rock with their legs, then leapt back into the boat, hunching low. I saw, from my hiding spot beneath the captain's bench, that Moses's arms were outstretched over our supplies, holding the braided vines that kept them tied down in the bottom.

The boat seemed to stand on end in the water, pushed back so far that we were almost flipped over. I felt my claws start to give way, and I moved slowly face-first to the back of the boat. Then I turned about and scrambled the other way, up the boat as she climbed the wave! Somehow the gust in our sail and the push and the captain's oars were enough—we went straight up and over the huge wave, splashing down on the other side with a loud thunk that rattled the teeth in my head and left me crouching under the captain's bench, shaking and soaked to the skin.

"We've done it!" the captain cheered. "Men, we've done it."

Moses and Chippy looked waterlogged and exhausted, and I noticed that Chippy's eye patch was off. I'd never had a good look at what lay beneath, and now I couldn't resist creeping closer to him to have a view. The men laughed and slapped each other on the backs, breathing hard and shaking off the water.

Moses motioned to Chippy quietly, saying, "You've lost your patch."

Chippy's hand quickly went to his eye before I could see much, but what I did see was enough—a red, puckered scar where an eye should be. Though the black fabric was menacing, what was beneath was worse.

"Have this," Moses said. He bit the bottom of his shirt and tore off a long strip of fabric, which he wound over Chippy's head, tying it tightly behind. Chippy looked too thankful to speak, so he just nodded at his mate, and they both turned to take in the view behind us: the breakers cresting white over the black rocks, and just beyond them the green gem of an island that we had called home for so many weeks.

"Are we all together, men?" the captain asked, looking over the stores in the bottom of the boat. I paced back and forth, inspecting everything, even the round brown fruit shells that Moses had filled with fresh water, and meowed to the captain that all looked well; nothing had been lost in our journey over the waves. Moses checked the rigging and said the same. "Then we set sail," the captain said quietly. He secured the rope in his hands by tying it off on the bench, then angled the sail where he desired.

The men were quiet for most of our first day back at sea, watching as our island slipped away behind us into a green dot on the horizon, then disappeared altogether. For a long while, no one spoke. Finally Chippy said quietly, "My lady will never let me go to sea again if I get out of all this."

Moses said his would feel the same, but that their young ones were grown now and he had no life other than to sail with the captain. I lay in the captain's lap and looked up into his face, handsome and tanned after our time on the island. I could tell he was thinking of Melissa—maybe, too, of the woman in that portrait he'd had in his quarters. But he did not speak. He was still the captain, and these were the men who served him.

The men spent the day steering the boat in what they thought was the best direction, based on where the captain believed our island to have been located. When the sun finally sank low into the waves, they studied the stars carefully over our heads and adjusted the sail as best they could. "This little boat will either take us home or bring us into the path of another packet ship," the captain explained of his course. After a light dinner of dried fish and fruit, we tucked in for the night, listening to the waves lap against the side of our small boat. I curled against the captain's side, happy to be back on the sea that I knew and loved so well. I slept soundly: no crashing rocks, no old bones, just our boat, my best mates, and the waves and stars to guide us.

CHAPTER 23

READING THE SKY

Our first days at sea were good ones, with wind in the sail and mostly clear skies. The fresh fruit began to go soft, and the men had to toss some overboard—not a problem for me, as I never cared for any of the bitter fruits the island had to offer. The water still tasted fresh, and we had enough fish to last for days.

The men kept up spirits by playing the tile game Chippy had fashioned from shells, and by telling yarns. The captain had also brought my island toy, and I was delighted to have it aboard: a dead beetle, dried by the sun and tied to a thin vine. Its shiny shell was great fun to chase through the boat as the captain tossed it to me, then quickly dragged it back before I could catch it. Sometimes I was too fast for him and did catch the shiny creature in my paws, but I was always careful not to use my sharps with the toy, as I did not want to damage it, and this took great restraint.

Moses had also brought a bit of the tincture he'd made for the captain's leg, and I watched as he unwrapped the bandage. "It's a wonder," Moses whispered, inspecting the wound. It was now almost completely healed: a large red scar covered the spot where the bone had once broken through, but all the blackness was gone, and the captain reported that it gave no pain.

"Mr. Moses, I owe you my life," the captain said quietly. "And you as well, Mr. MacNeil."

Moses only nodded, saying nothing as he wrapped the captain's leg in a fresh strip of cloth and secured it. I thought back to the island and the skeleton bones I had seen there. The memory brought a shiver down my spine. I was glad to know that now the captain would not end like that poor, unfortunate soul.

That evening the wind picked up, and the men were happy to have our small sail filled with air again. When Moses served our fish dinner, I found that it did not agree with my stomach. Instead I paced the boat as the sun sank behind the clouds. I tried to lie next to the captain after dark, but restlessness overtook me. My stomach growled, and I went to find the fish head I'd been left. After a few bites I didn't want more. I walked the length of the boat, back and forth, back and forth, stepping gingerly over the men as they talked into the night. I scratched behind my ears and gave myself a quick bath, but nothing could settle my nerves. It was as if something was moving under my fur. At last I took to digging my nails into the bottom of the ship, scratching away.

"Quit that racket, cat," Chippy growled, and brushed me away with his foot. Moses was telling a yarn, and the men wanted to listen, but I had no interest in their sea stories on this night. As I crossed the ship, I felt a funny vibration in my paws that stopped me. I stood still and let the feeling wash over me, as terrible as it was. It was oddly familiar, but it took a moment for me to place the feeling: It was the one I'd had on the *Melissa Rae* that morning, with my mother by my side, the day she died. And again, later, when we were put out into the longboat. A storm was coming!

I jumped onto the captain's chest, startling him. I meowed and pawed at him, jumping down quickly to set my claws into the wood. Then I remembered the sign my mother had taught me, and drew my paw across the wood slowly, three times. The captain held up one hand for Moses to stop his story, and looked to the sky. No stars were visible, as the dark clouds blocked even the moon. He took a deep breath and put his hand over the side of the boat, into the water, then held his fingers up in the air over his head, turning to and fro.

"What is it, Captain?" Moses asked.

"Foul weather. Let's put our sail at the southwest," the captain ordered.

"Southwest, Captain?" Moses questioned, sounding very tired. "That's the way we came—you mean to go backward?"

"Yes, I mean to go backward; we're headed dead into it,

from what I can gather, and we need to turn about until she passes. Then we can continue on."

Chippy did as he was told and adjusted the sail, but I could hear him and Moses talking quietly about "no drops yet" and good winds. I made my mark again, pulling my paw back on the wood to show them that I meant it, that I felt it. The captain pulled me into his lap and petted down my back.

"Good work, Jacob. You've done well," he said, staring out over the horizon, watching the dark clouds slowly move.

When the men had checked our stores and settled onto benches for the night, I knew there would not be much sleep. Moses threw me a bite of fish, but I ignored it. "How do we know he's not just off his food?" Chippy growled, looking at me. "He might be peaked."

"He's a fine cat, Captain, but pardon me for saying . . . he's no Mrs. Tibbs," Moses added. "Perhaps we stay the course and turn about if we see something amiss by morning light—or feel even one drop of rain."

The captain kept his hand on my back, and I could feel the tension run through him. "I've sailed many years, and on many ships, some of them with a fine crew, and some with lesser men. I've seen sea cats come and go. A few lazy and fat, who lay on the deck. Those that worked themselves lean catching rats. But none were as Mrs. Tibbs." He paused for a moment, as if to gather himself. "Mistakes I've made—and plenty to last me a lifetime. But ignoring that lady when she gave fair warning is perhaps the greatest mistake of my life. And to think I did it for profit, for speed! What it earned me was the opposite."

I saw Moses bow his head, perhaps thinking of Sean, or of Slattery and my mother.

"I lost two men their lives. I lost my ship, and her crew. And Mrs. Tibbs." Here he paused to run his hand down my back. "But I will never be that man again, the man who chose profit over the safety of his crew. As long as I am fit to command, I assure you that I will get you both safely home again, if it's the very last thing I do." The captain looked from Moses to Chippy and back again, but neither man had anything to say.

As if on cue, I felt a raindrop hit my back just then, followed quickly by another. The night stretched long and dark, with drops on and off, as if we were racing just ahead of the storm, at its edge. The men slept, as they could, between squalls, until along the horizon a thin pink line formed. "Red sky by morning," I heard Moses whisper.

"Sailor take warning," Chippy answered. He pulled hard on the rope that secured our meager sail, and tied it into place, sending our boat farther in the direction that the captain had ordered.

CHAPTER 24

FOUR MITTENS

By the time the light of day should have been over our heads, we were still wrapped in darkness, bouts of hard rain coming and going as clouds passed over us.

"Chasing us, she is," Moses said, huddled under his shirt, the collar turned up. It seemed impossible to escape the driving rain when it came, and the men were all sitting in damp clothes. I sat beneath the captain's bench and tried my best to clean my fur, but it was ruffled by the wind and would not obey me.

"We should have sailed through, kept course," Chippy mumbled, as if to himself.

The captain's face was grim, his mouth a thin, tense line. Did he doubt himself? Did he doubt me?

"What did I tell you, Moses, about that cat? Four mittens. I knew he'd be bad luck, and look where we are now," Chippy said. It seemed like he could be joking, but maybe not. Maybe he really did blame me.

Moses glanced over at me, his brown eyes sad, but he said nothing in my defense. I thought back over the journey since we'd left Liverpool, now months ago. I had to agree with Chippy; it had been nothing but bad luck followed by more of the same. A storm, the loss of lives, the captain's grave injury, a mutiny. But how could all of this be my fault, just because I had white paws?

I came out from under the bench and slowly crept to the captain's lap, hoping to find some solace there. But his hand did not find my back; instead he sat and watched the sky as more dark clouds rolled over us.

Maybe Chippy was right. I had never been a great ratter, and I hadn't been able to catch fish on the island. And I clearly wasn't able to read the waves like my mother had. Now I had surely turned our little vessel in the wrong direction; we would never outrun this storm and should have sailed through. Who knew if our longboat would survive it? I was a failure. Four mittens indeed! I jumped down from the captain's lap and curled into a ball under the bench, in a dark, damp corner. I shivered there, hungry and cold and ashamed. What my mother would think of me now, I did not want to know. I thought of my brave, strong brothers and sisters, picturing them to a one standing on the decks of great ships. I did not know what I had done to deserve this life, an unlucky runt. But I hated the knowledge that I had brought my mates and the captain down with me.

When evening finally fell, Moses offered me a bite, but I wouldn't take it. Not that I wasn't hungry; my stomach growled as it hadn't since I was a little kitten. But I refused food on principle. I had earned nothing, and I would have none of their stores. As the men huddled in the driving rain, I felt the boat shift suddenly. It was Chippy on his feet, standing, almost overturning us.

"Cap, what's that yonder—a light? A light!"

The captain turned quickly, dropping the bit of dinner he was eating. "I believe you're right, Mr. MacNeil. Moses, have a look."

In the excitement I came out and put my paws on the side of the boat, longing to see. What did a light on the waves mean? Was it from the storm or some type of fish? On our previous journey in the longboat, we had, in the dark of night, seen a glowing jellyfish at times, under the water. But this light, I saw quickly, was not bluish in tone as those sea creatures were. Instead it was a warm yellow, and it bobbed far off on the horizon, as if above the sea.

"It's a vessel, I know that it is! We're saved, mates; we're saved at last!" Moses picked up oars and began to row furiously in the direction of the glowing ball, and Chippy picked up the other set of oars. The splash of their rowing and jubilant calls rang out over the sea as I watched from my vantage point at the front of the boat. Could it be, finally, some good luck for us?

"Ho there, ho there!" the captain called out as we neared the light. "We hail from Liverpool, the *Melissa Rae;* I'm her captain, Nicholas Natick! Ahoy! Is anyone on watch?"

The ship came toward us, and grew before our eyes

from a dark shape to a full vessel, lit by several lanterns. She was four-masted, larger than the *Melissa Rae,* and rode heavy in the water, as if her hold was full. Finally, movement on the deck as a man called down, "Ho there! Ahoy!"

Our longboat suddenly seemed very small indeed as we pulled into a space beside the big ship. We could not see up to the deck, as it was too high over our heads, but we saw as ropes were lowered down to us, and men's faces appeared over the side, calling, "Ho there, sailors!"

"They speak the Queen's English; we are indeed saved men." The captain treated us to a rare smile. When the ropes were low enough, the men tied them to either side of our boat, and we were at once lifted from the waves, pulled in yanking starts and stops, until we were even with the gunwale of the great ship. Hands reached over the side for the men, and they were quick to pull themselves up. I watched, pacing the bench, waiting for someone to remember me in the longboat. As the men set foot on the deck, I started to mew. The distance was too great for me to leap. I was afraid I would slip between the longboat and the side of the ship, go down into the dark waves of the storm over our heads, and never be seen again.

I watched as the captain removed his hat, held it to his chest, and explained our situation to the other captain and crew. He told it quickly, in short terms, and I caught only a few of the words: a storm, mutiny, put out to sea, the Archer Shipping Company. Chippy and Moses stood at either side of our captain, as straight and brave as they could. Finally the great man of the ship nodded, and put his hand onto Captain Natick's shoulder with much sympathy.

I meowed again, forgotten and left behind in the longboat. Then I remembered Chippy's comments about me, my four white paws, how I was bad luck, and I stopped my crying. Had I been left in the boat not by accident, but by intention? Perhaps they were done with me! I crouched low and darted, using all the strength left in my haunches, and launched myself from the boat and onto the deck of the ship, where I landed, I'm proud to admit, on all four paws—perhaps with a bit of a skid.

My timing could not have been better, as I broke up a solemn discussion between the captains of maritime law, and of whether there had been any sight of the *Melissa Rae* since we were last aboard hcr.

"We put in to North Africa about that time, if your calendar of events is correct, and would not have passed her coming back this way," the head of ship said, just as I skidded by his feet. "What's this?" He leaned down to get a better look, and put his hand onto my back. "You have failed to introduce us to this most important crew member."

"Yes, this is Mr. Jacob Tibbs, my fine sea cat." Captain Natick smiled. "He's pleased to have his paws on deck, Captain Goldney, to be sure. I am hoping an animal on board is not a breach of your policy?"

"Indeed not, quite the contrary, as we have our own ship's cat, not to mention the cook's sow, who lived below on our journey out. My ship is friendly to animals, rest assured." Captain Goldney smiled down at me. I took in his dark eyes and trim mustache, and I liked his appearance instantly.

"Speak of the devil and he will appear!" one of the mates said. I smelled a strange scent—not quite that of a rat, but of fur and animal. And then, before I could react, a creature was before me: a huge tabby with brown-and-black fur, at least three times my size and as thick and fluffy as a down pillow. The cat froze, startled to see another of his species on board, then stepped to me quickly to size me up. One look in his cold green eyes told me he did not care for Captain Goldney's hand on my back, not a bit.

"See that, they will be fast friends, no doubt." Captain Goldney scooped up the big cat before he could reach me and cradled him in his arms. But the cat's eyes stayed locked on mine in pure hatred. He turned his head and hissed, scrambling from his captain's arms with full claws out and jumping back down to the deck.

"Leo Bear is his name, as we are quite sure he's either part lion or part bear—we aren't confident of which!" the captain went on, speaking quietly, as if he did not want Leo Bear to hear. "He's not exactly a friendly pet, but he does keep the ship free of vermin." The captain brushed some fluffy fur from his navy jacket. He was obviously a man who took pride in his dress, as he was on deck in a suit of pressed navy and shined boots, a hat upon his head and his shirt starched and white.

I glanced back to my captain and noted the state of his own appearance: His once carefully shaved face now had a week's worth of stubble upon it. His hat—held to his chest—once a fine wool, was now tattered and had lost its shape. His jacket was faded and torn, the elbows stitched together with Moses's handiwork on the island. "Our own Jacob was learning to become a good ratter himself, but his real trick is forecasting," the captain bragged. "It was he who warned us of this storm, and we turned about. We would never have found your ship without him."

Captain Goldney raised an eyebrow and looked down at me again. "A weather sphinx, is he? Then I'm all the happier to have him on board. I did wonder at how your vessel had survived the storm we just sailed through, as I could see no way out of it, so he must be a lucky cat indeed."

I felt pride well up inside my chest at the captain's words. Did he really credit me with saving the crew? My happiness was short-lived, as I noted Leo Bear approaching cautiously again to stand at his captain's side and preen his long fur. He was a magnificent cat, and I felt puny and small in his presence, even with the captain's compliments still hanging about my head.

I moved to stand next to my own captain's leg, and I took in the other crew lined before me: healthy and tan, clean and well dressed all. What an appearance we must have been in contrast! Chippy with his makeshift eye covering. Moses, a small man to start with and now made even smaller by the towering strong men of the other crew, his head bald while they all had thick braids and looked many years his junior. Our captain, with his cane of island wood and severe limp from his injury, a broken man with no ship to his name. And rounding out our crew, myself: a yellow-and-white runt, with four white paws, in the presence of an enormous cat with huge black paws and the name of Leo Bear! We were castaways indeed—castoffs was more like it, unwanted and broken, one and all.

"Let's show your men to quarters, where they can wash and have hot food to eat," Captain Goldney finally said, his hand on Captain Natick's shoulder again. "After a spell, we can meet in my rooms to set your story into the log, if you feel ready to do so."

"Indeed, your kindness is most welcome, and I cannot adequately express our gratitude," Captain Natick answered. The men turned and moved to the captain's quarters, with the sailors leading Chippy and Moses toward the galley. I had been forgotten again, left to stand on the deck with only the massive ball of fur called Leo Bear staring at me. I felt his cold green eyes rove over my form as he paced around me slowly, this way and that, as I stood stock-still. He seemed done with his evaluation, and moved to walk away, but then, quickly, he crouched low, leaning in to hiss in my face. But I did not falter, standing my ground as the larger cat towered over me. Seeing I would not flinch, the bear cat lost interest, turned, and with a swish of his puffy tail followed his captain into the warmly lit quarters.

When I knew he was safely gone, I let out a sigh of relief. Perhaps I had passed a test of bravery and the giant cat would leave me be. I leapt up to the quarterdeck and higher still, to have a look into the windows where my captain sat with this Goldney fellow. The room was washed in a yellow light from beautiful lanterns—unlike those aboard the *Melissa Rae*, these had colored glass that cast a warm glow. The captain's furnishings were equally fine, with red velvet chairs and a silky daybed lining one wall.

Captain Natick was offered a cup of tea from a silver tray in a white china cup, and took it greedily into his rough and dirty hands. I watched as he drank it eagerly, his hands shaking as he told his story—our story—to Captain Goldney, who wrote each word down with an ink pen into a leather-bound journal.

CHAPTER 25

LEO BEAR

After hiding from Leo Bear for a good portion of the evening, I found my way to the forecastle and, by scent, to my mates Chippy and Moses, where they slept in hammocks among the other sailors. I leapt up to Moses and curled in beside his chest, making myself small. When his hand found my back, I purred loudly. "There, there," Moses whispered. "You're safe aboard, little man."

I peered around in the dark to see if the giant cat had followed me, but he seemed the type to sleep in his captain's quarters or maybe in my favorite spot—beneath the stove in the galley. Or perhaps, if he was the ratter his captain claimed he was, he spent his nights patrolling the hold. I cared not what he did, as long as he did it far from me. I curled in tighter against Moses, listening to his soft snore, and pledged to not leave the side of my mates until we reached home again, as I suspected Leo Bear was aching to get me alone and make mincemeat of me.

In the dawn, I was awake and on deck by four bells on the morning watch, as the sun rose over the ship. I followed Moses and Chippy into the galley, my first glance at the room. I'd not had any food for almost a day—having been forgotten the night before—and hoped that today there would be something in a bowl for me. As we entered the galley, the sailors of the *Bristol* stood and cheered for the men, saying, "Ho! Welcome aboard!" Sailors never clapped on a vessel, as it might anger the god of thunder, Thor, but they would happily bang metal cups with silverware and make all manner of noise otherwise when the occasion arose. It was nice to feel that we belonged, but lodgings were tight and chairs were hard to come by. Two able-bodied men stood and gave way to my mates, and I leapt onto Moses's lap at the first opportunity.

"Our Leo can't be too fond of him," one of the sailors laughed, pointing at me.

Another chimed in, "He's the size of some of our rats, he is! Is he a regular cat, or some special breed?"

"He's just small—a runt," Chippy grumbled, chewing on a hardtack biscuit that the cook offered him. I could tell he was not too happy to be put in a position to defend me. I couldn't help but wonder if Chippy might like me better if I were the size of Leo Bear.

"He's still a kit," Moses added, patting my back. "And his journey has not been an easy one, to be sure."

"Aye, tell us how you came to find yourselves in that longboat," a young sailor said, and Moses launched into a short version of our tale, starting with the storm that hit the *Melissa Rae* and ending with our escape through the breakers of the island. I knew that by forenoon watch our story would be all over the ship, passed from sailor to sailor, with embellishments along the way, no doubt. I puffed up with pride when Moses mentioned my parts of the story—how I had warned of bad weather and the captain had turned the boat about, finding the *Bristol* in the end.

The group of sailors left to work their shift, leaving just my mates and myself in the galley along with the cook, who was called Colin. He was as round as Moses was thin, with a bushy head of blond hair that would not stay in a braid. When he tied on his smock over his clothes, his belly looked so high and round, I wondered if he was hiding a whole barrel beneath the cloth. "How would you care for a bit of grub, little one?" Colin offered me a piece of dried meat and a bowl of salty broth, which I quickly pounced upon.

"For one so small, he has a certain appetite!" Colin laughed, watching me. I noticed that Moses was already at work clearing the table and setting up washing, as he had done aboard the *Melissa Rae*. "That's my duty, sir; you can rest," Colin said, motioning for him to sit.

"As glad as I am to find myself back in a fine galley, it is my pleasure," Moses explained, and the *Bristol* cook nodded his understanding. Together the men washed and dried the cookware at the counter while I finished my meal. While they worked, they spoke of ways to make supplies last on a long journey, and how to put together a decent meal for the sailors. It was quickly decided that Moses's expertise would come in handy as we neared port and ran lower and lower on supplies. He and Colin would take on cooking together, and were happy to do so.

While I was distracted chewing on my salt pork, Chippy left the galley and went up on deck. I found him at the foremast, inspecting some issue with the stays. As I watched, he explained a repair to the young sailors gathered round him, then asked for tools to be brought.

While Chippy made repairs above, and Moses set to work below, both captains came on deck to take the air, walking in stride. Captain Goldney looked even more splendid in the light of day than he had the evening before, in a trim navy suit and shined shoes. Though Captain Natick leaned heavily on his cane and his limp was quite pronounced, it was clear that he had made an effort with his appearance as well, his trousers brushed clean, his tattered jacket over a fresh shirt—perhaps borrowed from Goldney.

Captain Goldney inspected the work of his sailors with a critical eye. Though the deck looked shipshape to me, nothing seemed to meet his expectations. "Whose work is this?" he yelled, checking the paint on the jolly boat and seeing some brushstrokes along the side. When he found the young sailor responsible, he handled him roughly by the arm and ordered him to "do over what you could not do right, and stay on deck through the next watch."

The boy kept his eyes down as he accepted his hazing, saying only, "Aye, Captain."

They took no notice of me as I sat beside Chippy while he went about his work, though Captain Natick stopped to inquire as to how he'd slept and if he was faring well. "I am well, Cap; good to be aboard again," Chippy answered.

"It is indeed," Captain Natick agreed. He seemed aloof and distant, not as he had been these past weeks. It took me but a moment to realize the change and why it had come about: The captain of any ship was above his men; they were not his mates, not his friends or comrades. They worked for him, and he was the master. All of that had altered when we were set to sea in the longboat, our misfortune being a great equalizer. Then we were one and the same, battling the elements on the sea and land. But now we were back aboard a sailing ship, and Captain Goldney obviously ran his crew tightly. Captain Natick had to fall in line with him, no matter what had transpired aboard our longboat—our roles from the *Melissa Rae* were resumed, as if they had never been broken.

I realized, too, what this meant for me. I was a ship's cat—and just as Chippy showed his abundant skills at woodworking, and Moses his in the galley, to earn their keep, I should show mine. I stepped away from Chippy while he continued his task and moved to the front of the ship, out the bow to the cathead. There I took in the sea below me as it rushed by. Chip was right, it was good to be aboard again. Though this ship and crew were different from the *Melissa Rae,* just having sails above and sea beneath made me at home, made me feel myself again.

I closed my eyes and took in my senses, trying to feel the approaching weather. After a moment or two nothing came to me—no sick lurch in my stomach, no shiver up my paws. We had fine sailing weather, and if my sense was right, it would continue for days steady on.

I opened my eyes again and had the shock of my life, almost tumbling overboard, when I saw that Leo Bear had come up alongside me, silently. The large cat stood close by, watching me intently through squinted eyes. Perhaps he was wondering at what I was doing. From what I had overheard he was strictly a ratter, and did not possess my skills for reading the sky and waves. Being raised as I was, by my gifted mother, I had assumed all sea cats could predict the weather for their mates, and give fair warning. But I now realized that while Leo Bear was large and strong, he had not been born on a ship, as I had. He was probably intended to be a cat for laps, with his long, luxurious fur and handsome looks, and not meant for the waves. I wondered why his captain had brought him on board at all, other than to catch rats (which any cat can do). Before I could ponder it much longer, Leo turned, swished his fluffy tail at me, and walked away. He went only a few paces before he stopped and turned, as if watching to see if I had followed. He waited, glaring, until I left my post and fell tentatively into step behind him.

The big tabby led me, as I somehow knew he would, to the hatch of the hold. Though I did not shiver at the thought of the weather, I did now, looking down into the dark dampness of below. Did the large cat mean to lead me to his lair? Leo Bear went down first, fast and easy. I followed behind him, getting a feel for the wooden ladder that led down into the underbelly of the ship.

The hold here was much like that of the *Melissa Rae*, packed from wall to wall with crates and parcels. But one sniff told me this was not gunpowder and rolled cloth she was holding. The ship had been to Spain and parts of northern Africa, and she carried back to England a cargo from there—delicious-smelling teas and spices, finely woven rugs, and ivory. Leo Bear disappeared into the darkness in front of me as I sniffed at crates and boxes filled with scents that had never crossed my nose before.

There was one smell in the hold that was pungent, and overwhelmed everything else—a scent of cold, of wet. It reminded me, a bit, of a fast-moving, eel-like creature I had encountered on the island. This, Moses had told me, was a snake, a very dangerous critter, and I should steer clear of it. Though it had looked like not much more than an eel on land, I'd obeyed his warnings.

I looked up to see Leo Bear perched by a strange dome-shaped package; I did not recognize what it was. He sat atop a wooden crate, next to a cage of close-set golden bars. The cage itself was a thing of beauty, so fine were the bars, and set so near each other that they sparkled in the dim light of the hold like rays from the sun.

I leapt up to get a closer look and was startled to see things moving inside, sliding about—like slippery tails or eels, only these were thinner, sleeker, and not under the

waves. Snakes! Unlike the one small snake I had seen on the island, these were huge, and a whole horrid pile of the things, writhing about, I could not even count how many.

Leo Bear looked at the cage proudly, then batted at the bars with his paws. The movement seemed to motivate the creatures inside, and they slid close to us, mouths open, hissing. I leapt back in fear, but Leo stayed on, pawing at the cage, perhaps knowing that the snakes could not reach him. They lunged but hit the gold bars from inside—hissing and spitting all the while.

How horrible they were! I spun on my paws and raced back to the ladder and up to the light of the warm deck, away from the darkness and the creatures below. I had no desire to see them again. It did not seem as though Leo Bear needed any help with ratting, so I decided to keep to above deck for the remainder of the journey—I had seen enough of the *Bristol*'s hold to give me nightmares.

CHAPTER 26

GREEN-EYED CAT

The next few days aboard the *Bristol* passed without incident, as I stayed within reach of my mates every moment, and as far from Leo Bear as I could manage. Chippy worked with the *Bristol* crew and proved himself as the skilled carpenter we all knew he was. As this ship had no carpenter of her own, Chippy made repairs that were wanting, and fixed the makeshift work that other sailors had done along the way. There seemed to be no competition there; the *Bristol* sailors respected his work and did not criticize.

Moses spent his days in the galley, trading yarns and getting along quite well with the *Bristol* cook, Colin. They were as two old mates, one lean and one plump, and turned out meals that the sailors talked up and down the ship as excellent and well flavored. Moses seemed happy again, though I never did see him repeat the trick with his tattoos that he had done for us when we were on the longboat. I wanted him to make the mermaid dance and show Leo Bear how delightful my mates were, despite our shabby appearance, but he did not. Perhaps it brought back too many bad memories, best forgotten. When I was sure that Leo was not by the stove, being near Moses in the galley was my favorite spot. I curled up there and rested, listening to the talk of the sailors as they came and went for meals and tea. And Colin usually found a pork rind or fish soup for me, adding, "He's not much for catching his own, is he?"

Moses shook his head. "He was just learning the ways of a ship's cat when we were put out . . ." He trailed off, as if to talk about that day was hard. "He was weaned on fish-head soup and has a taste for it—never did take to vermin."

"No matter. He's a handsome cat, and truth be told"—Colin dropped his voice—"I prefer him to the captain's."

Moses raised his brows but made no comment as Colin went on. "That ball of fur is not a friendly cat like yours here. And he leaves a wake of hair wherever he goes! I've had it in my dish before. This fine young fellow"—he motioned to me—"neat and clean, no muss and no fuss. And no hissing, either."

When the men filed in for meals, I listened to their talk and learned much about the history of the *Bristol* and what sort of ship she was. The crew was quite young, having only been out on one or two trips under the captain. The ship herself had been hired from England to the north of Africa, and back again. She had sometimes been used, I heard with shock, to move illegal cargo between the continents as well, going round to America before heading back to England. I noted that Chippy and Moses made no comment when this fact came up; Chippy only quietly ate his grub and kept his eyes on his plate. Perhaps he did not want to judge the men who had taken us in, saved us from the sea.

When I spied Leo entering the galley, I would quickly leap to my feet, move around him in a big circle, and dart up to the deck. If Chippy was not about, I would jump to the quarterdeck to spy in the windows of the captain's quarters. When they were open, I could see what the two captains were about. On one such afternoon, at about four bells, I found them tinkering with a metal device shaped like a *V* with maps spread all around them.

I listened through the open window as they spoke. "I believe we were off the coast of Spain, perhaps a bit further out than the Azores," Captain Natick said. He held a magnifying glass over the maps, looking closely at the charts of sea and land.

"How can that be? There are no lands yet discovered west of those, unless . . ." Captain Goldney held his metal measuring device over the maps and took down some notes. "If you strongly believe that this was your location, I have no answer but to suspect you and your men found new land."

The captain called for Chippy to enter the quarters, and he did, holding his hat in his hands. He, too, looked over the maps and consulted Captain Goldney's device, but the men could seem to come to little conclusion. I nestled down next to the window, listening to their conversation and the wind in the sails, dreaming of our island. What if we *had* discovered a new land? Would my mates recall that it was I, on that night, who'd spied it first? And would I be given the credit for it? The men had told stories before of great discoveries, of lands and oceans named for the men who first found them. An island, perhaps called Tibbs . . . I curled up and soon found myself dozing, dreaming of how my mother would beam with pride—her son, an explorer of new lands!

I woke to the sound of hissing, my eyes darting open. I expected to see Leo Bear standing over me, as he often did when I was asleep, watching me, studying my every move. But he was not there; I was alone, still next to the window of the captain's quarters, in the dim light of late afternoon. The weather was fine, and the wind strong in our sails. Perhaps I had imagined the sound, fearful as I was of Leo. I stood to stretch and move from the shady side of the quarterdeck to finish my nap in the sun when I took in a strange sight. An eel was laid before my paws on the deck. At least, I thought it to be an eel. But as I lowered my nose, it lunged at me!

Not an eel, but a snake! One of the terrible reptiles from below! How had it escaped from the golden cage? I stepped back carefully, gingerly, on delicate paws. The snake lifted its head slowly, so slowly, and locked eyes with me, moving forward, advancing on me.

I saw a movement from the corner of my eye as I backed

around the captain's quarters—Leo Bear. He stood, cleaning his paw, and glanced at me, with a bored expression that betrayed everything. That was when I knew: The snake had not escaped. He had brought it up, and put it next to me as I slept. The villain!

The hissing in front of me turned my head back to the creature. It slid along the wooden deck, advancing with a smooth, slippery movement to match my reverse steps. I stopped and faced him, in full view of Leo Bear. When the snake hissed again, I hissed back, crouching low. I continued to edge my way along the quarterdeck until I was out of planks—I would tumble backward onto the deck if I took one more step. There was nothing to do now but face the snake—or turn and run. One glance at Leo Bear decided my fate. I would not allow him the pleasure of seeing me turn tail and scurry to my mates. Not this time.

I tilted my head down, looking at the place where the snake's head seemed to meet its body. This was where I would usually bite and shake a rat or mouse to bring it to an end. But the snake did not have a clean line—his head and body seemed as one. Where to bite? Where to sink my teeth and claws in? And his skin was rough and scaled—so thick. How would I get hold and injure him at all?

I stepped back, instinctively, and felt my paw slide off the quarterdeck. I dug in my claws and inched forward, just enough to keep myself on sure footing. It occurred to me that I was in the position that the Gray One had been in, forced into a corner, as it were, with no way of escape.

On one side of me a venomous snake, on the other the fat ship's cat, watching with glee. I had to fight, whether I wanted to or not.

Suddenly the snake lunged at me without warning, turning its head sideways and snapping at my throat. I pulled back just in time to avoid its bite, and the snake recoiled, hissing. Now was my chance, my only chance. I remembered my fateful error the first time I jumped on a rat: leaving his jaws to snap. I would not make that mistake again with this dangerous creature.

I felt my haunches twitch, and then, all in one motion, I had my jaws locked at the base of its hissing head. I landed on the deck with the snake firmly in my bite, flipping it over to expose a long white belly. It twisted, oh how it twisted! Like a living coil of rope, its entire body seemed to roll over in my mouth, so I bit down harder, my paws holding it steady. I pulled back with my teeth, tugging and shaking, but the animal was rubbery, and bent with my shake instead of breaking. I would have to do more.

Reluctantly, I braced my paws on either side of my mouth and tore a bite out of the snake. It fought harder now, but I dug in my claws and went in for a second bite. The snake twitched as my teeth at last hit bone, and I held tight until I felt the bones begin to snap one by one.

I released my jaws and watched as the snake's limp, heavy body slid to the wooden planks. I poked the creature with my paw and felt its cold weight. Such a majestic animal, so quick and agile, now lifeless and heavy, like a wet rope. I heard another hissing beside me and spun around, afraid that I would find yet another snake to battle. But it was only Leo Bear, witness to the whole event, crouched low and angry. Did I have to now fight him as well? I was certain he had put the snake there for me to find—perhaps to bite me in my sleep! He had expected me to run away, as I had when he showed me the snakes in the hold. But I didn't. I fought. And I *won*. And now Leo Bear was furious. He growled, then turned, puffed up his tail, and marched away, down to the main deck, without a backward glance.

The lanterns were lit in the captain's quarters now, and I could see that the two men were still inside, consulting maps and reading books. I knew not what to do, so I picked up my kill and dragged it over to the door of the cabin. The body was heavy, unlike a rat that could be carried by its scruff. I dragged the whole length of it over to the cabin and scratched at the door to gain entry.

After a moment, the door opened and a yellow light spilled out over me. I blinked, and looked up into the face of Captain Goldney. "A visitor," he laughed. "Not the one I expected, though." He turned to Captain Natick. "I believe he's here for you. Come in, cat, you're welcome."

I turned to pick up the snake and heard a gasp. "My man, come quick! Your cat has caught . . . a snake?"

Captain Natick limped to Goldney's side as fast as his crutch would carry him, looking down at me. "Jacob, what is this you've found? And how have you managed it?"

Goldney took a lantern down from the mantel and

held it over my kill. "It's from the hold—these creatures are highly venomous, deadly, even. We're bringing them to a zoologist in London for his studies. Is your animal injured?"

My captain leaned to pick me up and inspected me roughly, turning me about and looking for marks. "He is not. Is the creature truly dead?"

Captain Goldney kicked the snake with his boot and it rolled, lifeless, exposing a white belly. "It is indeed. I'll send the sailors down to inspect the cage in the hold—if one has escaped, there may be more!"

Once orders were given, Captain Goldney put his hand to my back and petted me gently. "And here you said he was not much of a ratter. He's only caught a snake, and a venomous one at that!" I purred my happiness at being admired by two great men, and as I did, I happened to catch a sight I could not have planned for better: a flash of fur by the window, where Leo Bear had surely been watching. His plan to embarrass—or wound—me had backfired terribly. In this hour, I was the hero of the *Bristol,* and he was all but forgotten.

CHAPTER 27

HERO

I will, perhaps, never know how the clever Leo Bear managed to get that small snake from the cage without letting any others out. I guess that when there is a will—a strong will—there is a way, and Leo Bear was certainly a cat with a will of iron! From the talk I heard in the galley that night, the sailors checked the hold and found all the reptiles accounted for, save the one I had killed, so they had no explanation, either.

I was roundly lauded and celebrated the next day and night with a large bowl of fish-head soup from Colin and many strokes from the crew, including my own mates. Even Chippy pulled me into his lap and scratched me roughly behind the ears, saying, "You are your mum's boy at that, aren't you, Tibbs?" This compliment from our saltiest crew member was perhaps the best of all.

Leo Bear made himself scarce, and I did not see even a whisper of his tail for at least two days. This left me with plenty of time to enjoy the galley, as I used to on the *Melissa Rae,* warming myself by the stove and listening to my mates tell their yarns. There was always a bit of jerky dropped on the floor to chew on as well, which helped to keep my stomach full, and naps aplenty.

My days in the galley, basking in my own pride, were not all sunshine and smooth sailing, though, as I began to gather that trouble might once again await Captain Natick and my mates as soon as the *Bristol* reached port. When Chippy and Moses were out of earshot, the sailors talked of serious things: maritime laws, mutiny, and what happens to a captain who leaves his ship, or is forced off.

"There's no shipping company I know that will let it stand," one sailor told Colin. "Natick will be lucky if he's not thrown in the gallows when we reach land."

"He'd best hope that that vessel made good time, and is docked again in Liverpool or heavy with cargo on her way back," another young sailor of the *Bristol* chimed in. "Or it will be his head."

I tried to curl back into my nap beneath the stove, but the talk about Captain Natick bothered me and caused my stomach to ache. These sailors did not know what had occurred aboard the *Melissa Rae,* how Archer had treated us all, how truly insane he was. But I began to worry that others also wouldn't understand, and that somehow it would be perceived that Captain Natick and his men had done something wrong. Though I had looked forward to returning to dock at Liverpool, I now began to dread it. What fate awaited us there?

The next morn was gray and overcast, and I greeted it with my usual visit to the deck. There I heard a sailor at the top of the mainmast shout down, "Land ho!" We were but one day out from England and docking in Liverpool. I stood at the bow and looked out over the dark gray sea with a feeling of overwhelming sadness. We had left port so many months ago with my mother on board, and myself just a kitten. I was returning to land a different cat altogether, and alone.

Leo Bear chose just that moment to appear by my side. But instead of looking me over with a sneer and a hiss, he stood his distance and regarded me with something else—was it fear, or respect? Slowly he approached, humbled, his tail down. He paused a few paces from me, waiting for a sign. I searched my heart and found that I did not wish ill will between us, here at the end of our journey, and somehow I forgave him. I could not help but see things from his side. What if it had been the reverse, with the *Melissa Rae* rescuing a group of sailors who came aboard with their own captain's cat? How would I have felt to see Captain Natick, his hand on the back of Mr. Leo Bear, admiring him, upon the ship that I called my own? I, too, might have stung with jealously. I do not think I would have taken such a measure as releasing a venomous snake to test my foe, but still, I did understand his motives and now his regret.

I bowed my head and moved my tail gently, sending a sign to Leo Bear that he was forgiven, that all was well. He quickly and gleefully accepted, joining me. He stood beside me, taking in my pose and trying on the same stance. He looked out over the sea between us and Liverpool, perhaps trying to see what I saw. But I knew that while Leo had many gifts, he could not learn the ways of forecasting. I had been born with a special skill, passed on to me by my mother, and there was no way of teaching it.

Even with my triumph over Leo Bear complete, my melancholy mood hung about me like a wet sail. A storm was coming, I could feel it in my paws, but I also knew we would be well docked before it struck. After standing with Leo on the deck for a bit, I found my way to the galley and showed Moses and Colin the sign of weather approaching by scratching my paw across the wooden planks. Moses recognized it at once and went to tell the captain.

Though I knew I had done well by my mates to predict the weather, this was not a surprise storm—surely Captain Goldney knew the clouds well enough by now to see that rain was on the way. My special skills gave me no satisfaction; I was so worried for the captain and what might await him on shore. A different type of storm altogether.

The day passed in the usual way, but with the sailors now readying the ship for our arrival back at Liverpool. The mood on board was jubilant, the young men who served Captain Goldney happy to have home in their sights, the thoughts of their loved ones waiting for them on land. Moses and Chippy were also brightened, though a bit cautious—Moses to see his wife, and Chippy to see his, and his extended seafaring family as well.

We spent one more night aboard the *Bristol*, the men

in the galley up late singing and celebrating. Moses and Colin outdid themselves with biscuits and aged cheese, a sweetened duff, and dried meats—the rest of the stores on board put forth in a giant feast. They scraped the barrels and left only enough for breakfast. By midday next, we would be home.

I sat along the stove and noticed that Leo Bear slunk in to sit near me. The week before, I would have skittered out of the galley, my tail between my legs, at the mere sight of him. But not now. I had earned my right to be here with the sailors. I stayed my ground and resumed giving myself a bath, then joined Leo Bear, curling in for a warm nap, my back to his. This proximity was not lost on the sailors, as one called out, "Look at these two mates, thick as thieves!" I looked up to see Moses smiling down at us, happy that the two ship cats were finally friends.

I watched the sailors celebrate and felt a bit hollow inside—they played a game with cards and rolled dice and passed around a brown bottle. Even Chippy and Moses got into the act. It had been a long journey, with plenty of peril along the way. But as this was my first time out to sea, I knew nothing else, and I didn't feel like celebrating, not quite yet, not until I knew Captain Natick would be welcomed back on land. The thought of seeing Melissa again, though—her warm smiling face and blond curls—thrilled me. I wondered if she would be pleased with my growth, and what a changed creature I was! But even the joy of that reunion was tainted with sadness: I did not look forward to seeing her face when she learned the news that my mother was not with us. Oh, how sad she would be—my mother had been with Captain Natick since before Melissa's birth.

It seemed there was no escape from my dark mood. Every bright thing I could think of came with another side, too. I tried, instead, to think of all I had accomplished, how much I had grown, and how proud Mother would be of me, as I drifted off to sleep, my last night aboard the *Bristol*.

CHAPTER 28

THE DOCKS

As the sun broke over the deck the next morning, land was visible to all on board—not just the lookout with the glass up in the nest of the mainmast. The sailors who were not on duty spent their time in quarters packing up their belongings. I watched, inspecting each interesting item, as Chippy carefully put the tools he had been using away in a wooden box. He had no belongings at all, save for the clothes on his back and a new eye patch that Moses had sewn for him during our time on the *Bristol*.

I scurried down to the galley to see what Moses was busy with and found that he and Colin had quite a task before them, clearing the cabinets and storing all the serving plates and dishes. The ship would be at dock for only a fortnight before she put back out, and everything that could be ready was made ready before reaching land. "Goldney will be down to have a look, his second time in the galley this trip out," Colin explained. It seemed odd to me that the captain of the *Bristol* almost never set foot in the galley; obviously, he thought he was above it. On the *Melissa Rae*, Captain Natick was usually served meals in his quarters, but he took tea in the galley every day, checking in with his sailors and his cook.

When Captain Goldney did appear, I hid beneath the stove and listened to his stern inspection of the hold and the galley. First he hazed Colin for a broken tray, saying he would dock his pay if even one piece of silverware was missing. Then the man counted every piece, while Colin and Moses stood aside and watched. He found a knife missing, and a fork with bent tines. "You should lose five quid for that," Goldney said sternly. "But you will pay for it on the next trip, won't you?"

Though I knew from talk in the galley that Colin wished not to ship out with the *Bristol* next, he had signed papers with the captain and was tied to the ship for two more journeys. The captain meant to reduce his pay on the next trip, to make up for the tray and silver, which seemed rather unfair to me. But perhaps it was better to have docked pay than no pay at all—a fate that Moses and Chippy were facing, I feared. No sailor who left his ship midjourney would be paid by the shipping company that had hired him on, that was sure.

When Goldney moved to make his exit, I wanted to stay behind in the galley and console my mates, but something he said changed my mind. "A jolly boat will go ahead to see how they want to handle your lot." He nodded to Moses. "You're to stay below until I say you can leave the ship, is that understood?" The way he addressed the sailors was very different from how he spoke when Captain Natick was around.

Moses nodded his understanding, then caught himself and answered, "Yes, Captain."

I followed quickly in Goldney's footsteps and found myself on deck as he gave orders to two young sailors. He sent them in the jolly boat on ahead of the *Bristol*, to reach Liverpool before we would have a chance to dock. "And take this straight to the harbormaster," he said, pulling a folded piece of paper from his breast pocket and handing it to one of the boys. "Either stay ashore or come back directly, as he wishes."

I noticed that Chippy and Captain Natick were not on deck as the jolly boat was lowered into the water. Once the men were off, Captain Goldney spun and returned to his cabin, grabbing the arm of one young sailor he found who seemed not to be engaged in much work. "Boy, come along and pack my trunk," he ordered.

I watched as land grew closer and closer to us. The wind picked up, causing the waves to lap the ship in a frothy mix that changed from a deep navy to a gray-green as we neared the port. We were no longer out on the deep, but coming in over the reefs and sand that lay not too far beneath our ship. I had a looming feeling in my chest, watching the skyline of the port city appear. This was a place of men, and of laws, unlike the world I had been

living in. A ship is its own little country, and I wasn't sure I wanted to leave it just yet. Much as I had disliked Leo Bear, and much as I was beginning to dislike Captain Goldney, I preferred their company to that of the strangers and strange ways of landlubbers.

There was much maneuvering to be done as we entered the harbor, adjusting the sails and steering the large wheel to bring the ship in at the right angle and anchor her close. From there she would be pulled in by smaller boats and secured to the dock with ropes and anchor. The sailors, to a one, gathered on the deck to wave to land, yelling and hollering for their families who might be there, save for Moses and Colin, who had been ordered to stay below.

Captain Goldney stood nearest to the gangplank with Captain Natick at his side. My captain was hard to read, his face solemn and unsmiling, but I ran to him and wove myself through his legs in a figure eight. I noted with much glee that he did not have his cane, the one Moses had whittled for him on the island, and that he seemed steady on his own two legs. He moved with a limp, to be sure, but he seemed more able and looked more the part of a true captain. I sat beside him and looked out over the city of Liverpool as we were brought in.

"Lower the plank!" Goldney ordered as soon as we neared the huge wooden dock. Sailors leapt to work, securing lines and running up and down the gangplank as soon as it was close enough to dock. When we were tied up fast, Captain Goldney tucked one hand into his jacket front and marched down the gangplank in his shiny black boots, which I was certain his young cabin boy had been busy cleaning for hours the evening before.

It was not until I looked up into the face of my captain that I noted something was wrong. Captain Natick had gone pale beneath his tan, his skin taking on a gray hue. Yet he stood tall and brave, watching the events on the dock. I skittered to the hole by the gangplank to have a look myself, and saw several men talking to Captain Goldney. They wore long coats of navy with gold buttons all the way down the fronts, and odd rounded hats with a silver badge, very unlike the headwear of my mates. In their suits they looked rather serious, and the mood on board the *Bristol* grew hushed as we all gathered and watched the proceedings.

"Captain Natick, Captain Nicholas Natick?" one of the men in uniform yelled up to deck.

The captain stood for a moment, stock-still, then answered, "I am he." He moved carefully, perhaps to avoid the appearance of his limp, down the gangplank to join the men. He had barely set foot upon the dock when the men introduced themselves, then motioned for him to turn about. They took him by the arms and secured his wrists behind his back with something that looked like metal bands. The captain bowed his head, as if shamed. Who were these men? And what were they doing to Captain Natick? I knew not what was happening, only that all was not well and that my worst fears about reaching land seemed to be coming true.

I raced down the gangplank myself, unsure what else to do, and Chippy was quick after me. "What is the meaning? Do you know who this man is?" he hollered.

Captain Goldney turned his back to Chippy and said to the officers: "Another of his crew—Charles MacNeil, if I'm correct. He was second or third on the *Melissa Rae*."

As soon as the words were out of his mouth, the other uniformed man, a portly fellow, spun Chippy about and lashed his arms as well. But unlike the captain, who stood with his head bowed, Chippy spewed fire. Every curse I've heard a sailor utter came through his lips, and he yanked at his arms, fighting the man who held him.

"Your letter said there were three mutineers aboard?" the portly officer asked Goldney.

Captain Natick looked up and met Goldney's eyes, suddenly aware that his fellow captain, the man who had saved us from the waves, had informed on the crew of the *Melissa Rae* before we reached shore. That jolly boat he had sent ahead . . . the letter . . .

Captain Goldney gave no pretense of innocence. "Yes, the cook is below. He'll give no trouble; he's feeble," Goldney said, tapping the side of his head. I looked up at the man whom I had once thought a great sea captain. His fine clothes and handsome mustache now held no appeal, and I saw him for what he was: a traitor. Hearing Moses called feeble was the final straw for me, and I lunged at the horrible wretch, attacking the only bit of him I could reach: his precious boots. I laid claws into them, and teeth, scratching deep and long into the fine, soft leather, leaving marks that no shine or polish would be able to get out. Goldney kicked at me, so I clawed up his leg, causing the officers to laugh.

"That's a mad animal—he yours?" one of the officers asked. "Of your ship?"

"He is not!" Captain Goldney yanked me back by my nape and tossed me aside on the deck like an unwanted rag. He brushed his hands down his trousers to remove my fur and looked to his boots, noting the damage I had done. I assume I'm lucky he didn't simply drop me into the drink altogether. But perhaps if he had dropped me into the ocean, I would not have had to witness what came next.

Colin was ordered to bring Moses up from below, and, without further shackles or officers to be had, the *Bristol*'s cook was ordered to lead his new friend into the custody of the constable. To see Colin's face added only more heartbreak to an already terrible situation. I could barely watch as Moses was led off the ship, like an animal. But what came next was even worse: As the sailors began to file off, I saw Leo Bear in their mix. The scoundrel cat raced to his captain's side and was lifted in a wink. Captain Goldney held his huge, fluffy cat and petted him as if he were a prize to be treasured. Leo Bear looked down at me where I stood, puny and rumpled next to my bound mates. I vowed in that moment never again to be so quick to forgive a foe, for it was clear that while I had defeated Leo Bear on board the *Bristol,* his captain had won the war. It made me positively ill to see them together, content, while my own captain was led from the dock in shackles.

I moved to follow the men down the long wooden dock and found that my legs were not quite stable yet off the ship. I crouched low to make myself unnoticed and crept beside them as best I could. I heard the head officer explain the charges, though they made little sense to me, something to do with "abandoning ship," and for Chippy and Moses the charge of "mutiny." I did catch one bit that set my blood to ice: "She's not been heard of since; no ship has passed her. And she never arrived in port."

Captain Natick stopped altogether when he had this bad news. "She is lost at sea? The *Melissa Rae*? Is there truly no word, nothing at all?"

The officer holding the captain's arms shook his head. "The owner, Mr. Archer, Senior, is in rare form, you can imagine. His only boy was aboard that ship."

"He did not know how to sail," the captain murmured. "The second and third mates went with me . . ." He closed his eyes. "If they are lost, then God rest their souls, every one."

I thought back to my time on the ship and tried to imagine a voyage without the captain, without Sean, Moses, and Chippy aboard. Who would know how to navigate? And who would cook? We had all assumed they had reached New York Harbor, but perhaps they had not—they were a crew with no captain, no experience.

My thoughts went to young Bobby Doyle, who had stood with us and was left behind. Oh, what had happened to them at last? Was it a storm or something else? I had overheard the sailors saying that a ship with no cat on board was bound to be unlucky, and Archer had thrown me, the only cat left, over the side. Had that been their undoing?

I was pulled from my thoughts when a boot struck my belly. "Go on then, mangy!" One of the officers kicked me to the side as the dock turned into cobblestone streets. I tried to follow still, but he stamped his foot at me again and I startled, darting back onto the dock.

"That's our animal," Moses said, turning to Colin. "That's our ship's cat; can we collect him?"

"He's no use to you where you're going; leave him be," the portly officer said.

"I will come back for him," Colin promised my mates quietly. "I'll be sure to find him on my way round."

The captain said nothing, so preoccupied was he with the news of his ship, of the fear that all souls were lost. I did not know it then, but this would mean a more serious charge for him, both morally and legally. He had left his own ship, and without his steerage she was lost at sea with all souls aboard, a heavy weight indeed. I watched helplessly from the edge of the waterfront as my best mates and my captain were led away from me, into the busy teeming streets of Liverpool, going where, I did not know. I let out one small mew of complaint, though I assumed it would fall on deaf ears, such was the clatter of the busy street before me. But I glimpsed, just for a moment, Moses, his eyes looking back at me with worry. "Stay put, Jacob," he called to me as he was led away.

I turned and watched as the *Bristol* was being unloaded, the stores from her hold lifted onto the deck with ropes and pulleys. But when I caught sight of Captain Goldney and his horrible fat cat coming my way, I turned tail and ran, not caring where I was going, down the cobblestone street, hugging close to the curb, as far as the next dock. There I stopped, crouched down in the bustle of people and ships around me, to catch my breath. I tried my best to straighten my fur, but I felt wobbly and unsure of myself, perhaps just trying to get my land legs back. I was surrounded by all types of creatures and things I had never seen before, all kinds of activity, yet without my mates I felt more alone than I ever had.

CHAPTER 29

NO SHIP TO CALL HOME

The docks of Liverpool, I quickly learned, are no place for a little animal such as a cat. Though I had grown healthy and strong during our adventures at sea and on land, I was still young and undersized for my age. But even if I had been the size of Leo Bear, I would have felt small compared to the buildings and creatures I now found myself surrounded by. The docks themselves were huge—the *Bristol* was just one ship at port on the Coburn Dock, which was just one of many piers that spread like fingers from the city of Liverpool out into the ocean. I looked down the span of the dock before me and could count five ships in port—some bigger than the *Melissa Rae,* one even larger than the *Bristol*! I had never seen so many tall ships in one place.

The animals I had encountered thus far were limited to other cats, rats, snakes, of course, and the creatures I had seen on the island. Now around me were shapes and sizes of living things I could hardly comprehend. There were other cats—mostly a mangy lot, thin and with patchy fur, looking as though they'd been put out by their captains, or perhaps had never had a ship to call home. But there were other animals: dogs with leaking jowls and uncouth barks, horses with huge hooves and no mind of where they put them, and a variety of livestock that made up the rest. I noted, with added disgust, that most of the dogs wore collars around their necks, as if they did not possess enough smarts to remember their own names or where they belonged.

I wove my way down the dock on paws not quite accustomed to land, wobbling a bit and looking up at the majestic ships. Of course it was foolish to not be more aware with so much activity going on around me, as I learned almost too late! I darted to the side to keep from being struck by the quick feet of two horses pulling a cart full of wooden crates along the cobblestone street. Just then, the storm that I had sensed hours before began to show itself in the form of fat, cold raindrops. I remembered what Colin had said, that he would collect me, and I scurried back to the street and returned to the dock where the *Bristol* was secured.

I thought I would have no trouble picking it out from among the other ships, but as I made way down the dock, I grew confused. Around me, men and animals scurried to get out from the rain. Large canvas tarps were launched over carts carrying goods, and sailors battened hatches on board the ships. In the driving rain, I blinked hard and put my ears flat, trying to see a name or recognize any feature of the *Bristol.* But I was jostled to and fro by human feet and dashing horses and barking dogs, and finally I scurried up the nearest gangplank, hoping it was the *Bristol.*

I made my way up onto the deck of the ship, and realized, all at once, that it was not the *Bristol,* not even close, with only three masts. I jumped into a coil of rope I found on deck and curled in, out of the rain, to think for a moment. How would I find Colin again, and my way back to the captain and my mates?

Just then the coil around me began to unwind, and I looked up to see large hands over me. I leapt out, onto the deck and back into the rain, and found myself facing a stranger in sailor's clothes.

"Ah! A cat, huh! You'll be the death of me, scared me from my wits!" the sailor laughed. He reached to scoop me up, but I dashed from him, afraid. "Here, cat. Come on now." He reached again, snatching at my tail. There was something about him that did not agree with me, and so I ran, fast across the deck and down the gangplank, skittering along the dock and back to the streets of the wharf as quick as I could, minding the horses and carts as I went. When I reached the stone streets, the rain was still driving hard, with no sign of stopping. I wanted to sit at the end of Coburn Dock and await Colin's return, but surely he would stay out the storm wherever he was before coming for me? I sat until the rain had flattened my whiskers, watching as every other living creature in Liverpool, man or beast, found somewhere to get in out of the weather.

I looked about to see what shelter could be had, and saw what appeared to be a livestock building across the busy street. The large front door was open, and if I could reach it, there were sure to be plenty of places to hide within. But getting across was another problem altogether, with horse hooves flashing by in either direction at such a speed to make your head spin! I crouched low on my haunches and made to leap. The carts raced by me, their large wooden wheels splashing up mud and grit from the streets, which coated my fur as I scurried across, quick and low as a little mouse.

I made it to the middle of the street before I stopped, and here the traffic reversed, with carts and horses coming from the other way. I started across—too soon! I froze and let a cart pass over me, and I cowered between its wheels. Just as that cart rolled on, though, another horse followed it, and I sat directly in line of those hooves! I dashed, without looking, my eyes set on the barn across the way, and moved as fast as I could. When I reached the building, I was breathless and fairly covered in mud; one quick glance down at my front legs showed that I had been transformed from a handsome yellow-and-white cat to a plain brown one! I welcomed the rain now, though it did little to loosen the dirt from my fur.

I slunk through the tall open doors of the livestock building and took in an odor that did not agree with me.

Animals of all sorts were here, from rat to horse, and the place smelled of it. The space was big, with high ceilings and a tin roof through which the sound of the rain could be heard magnified several times over. The men who were working with the animals inside had to shout to be heard. The floor was covered in a soft coating of hay, which would have been lovely save for the occasional droppings of horse and cow that spotted it throughout. And these were not small droppings; the horses could easily leave behind a pile that towered over my head.

I made my way over to one side of the dark building and crept low, trying not to raise the attention of the men I saw around me. I hugged the stall doors with my side as I slid by, moving slowly and letting my eyes adjust to the darkness deep in the barn. Through the stall doors I could hear the snuffling of the animals within; I did not know if they were horses, cows, pigs, sheep, or something else. Between the rain overhead and the creatures snuffling and mooing and braying, the noise was overwhelming, but at least I was safe from the weather. I found a quiet corner, hid myself behind a pitchfork, and set to work giving myself a bath. My thoughts went to my mother, and what she might make of my current state: parted from my mates and walking the streets of Liverpool looking no better than the strays I had seen slinking about. At least my appearance was one thing I could set right, and that I did.

It took quite a long time to clean and tidy my muddy fur, and only afterward did I realize how tired I was. A bite of food would have been welcome, but I saw no way to have any of the feed that was given to the larger animals, and it would not suit my stomach in any regard, as it was all dry chow and hay and grasses. I might search for mice or rats, as there were certain to be some here, but I had never cared for the taste of them. I hunted them only out of duty. I felt the overwhelming weight of my current predicament settle over me, and suddenly I was so weary I could do nothing but curl in for a nap against the rough burlap, the sounds around me drowned out by my sadness. A vision of the captain was burned in my mind, his head bowed and his arms behind his back, as he was led, limping, away from me down the cobblestone streets of Liverpool. All the talk of the sailors aboard the *Bristol* had come to pass: my captain was in custody, and my mates as well. No matter how hard I tried, I could not see any way out of the mess we were in, and how we would ever set to sail again.

When I woke, the lanterns that lined the row of stables had been lit, and it seemed that the animals were asleep, or almost all of them. A few snuffs and scuffles could still be heard, but it was quieter than it had been earlier. The rain seemed to have let up as well, leaving me free to make my way back to the dock, to await Colin or perhaps my mates. I hoped I had not missed anyone during my rest, or during the storm. If I had, I would be forced to find the *Bristol* and possibly face that terrible Leo Bear again, something I did not welcome.

I came out from my hiding spot and stretched my back

and paws, making sure my fur was set straight before I moved to the sidewall and, crouching low, made my way for the door. "Aye there, mister, looking for trouble?" My paws froze as a voice reached me from across the barn. "We've plenty of mice that could use catching, for one who's not lazy. Come here, cat, let me see you. Don't be shy." An old man on the bench beckoned me, but I backed away. He didn't look dangerous, but I remembered the sailor aboard the ship who had snatched at me. I wanted to stay away from anyone who meant me harm.

"I've something here that might interest you," he called again, and I glanced over to see him dangle a fish by its tail. The meat had mostly been eaten away, leaving just head, tail, and a row of bones. It was perhaps his own dinner, and he was offering me the rest. My stomach rumbled with hunger at the sight, and my paws slowly padded to him, as if under a will of their own.

As I neared him, he reached out, and I flinched back. "Now, just an old sailor to another, saying how d'ya do," he said kindly. He laid the fish on a metal plate by his feet and motioned to me. I moved in closer again, pouncing on it. As I enjoyed my meal, I felt his fingers lightly scratch behind my ears. "Sailed with one as you, many years gone now!" the old man laughed. "This cat could tell the weather, he could! Old Blackie. Rest him, rest him well—a friend to sailors, he was." The old man puffed on a pipe of scented tobacco and petted my back, his mind obviously lost in thought.

As I finished the fish, he talked on, telling a story

of storms at sea, of great creatures he had seen, and an island girl he loved. He talked and talked, petting my back gently. When I had eaten all that I could, I stretched and licked my paws clean, noticing that the old sailor seemed to have drifted off to sleep.

I moved to the doors of the barn and looked out into the damp night, where a gentle rain still fell. Now there were no horses and carts on the road; the docks were empty of men, with just the huge ships bobbing gently on the waves. I looked back to the warmly lit stables and the old sailor now fast asleep with a blanket over his lap. Surely Colin would not come until morning to collect me. There seemed not a soul on the streets or the docks. I decided to stay in the barn until the sun rose; then I would go out and search for Colin, rain or no rain.

I returned to the boots of the old man and curled in against his blanket, cozy warm and tummy full. Perhaps all was not lost! Tomorrow would be another day; I would find Colin and then my mates. I felt my eyes close gently, listening to the sound of the old man's snuffled snores—a friendly reminder of the sailors' quarters aboard the *Melissa Rae*.

The next thing I knew, the early dawn filled the livestock stalls with dusty beams of daylight. As I stretched, I realized I was no longer on the old sailor's blanket, but instead had been put down on a mat of hay. My tail brushed something, and I turned, quickly, only to see a series of closely set lines behind me.

Bars?

I spun around and saw the same on all sides. I was surrounded by thin bars—not too unlike the cage that had held the snakes aboard the *Bristol,* only now it was I looking out instead of looking in!

I put my paw out between two of the bars and found that it fit easily, but only for a short distance. I used my claws to grasp the hay around me. But it was no use: I was trapped.

I began to meow for help. Perhaps the old sailor was still nearby and could get me out. How had I gotten into this mess? Had I fallen into a cage? Been trapped somehow? I paced the small space, digging up the hay at the bottom only to find more bars beneath me.

Finally, a shadow moved through the dawn light and approached. A man knelt down and I could see, quite close to me, the face of the old sailor—I was saved at last!

"Morning to you, sailor," he greeted me, then dangled a fish head over the cage, bones still attached through the tail. It was the same meal I'd eaten the night before, only remnants left now. "You must be ready for grub." I watched his fingers move over a metal latch, sliding it open, before he swung a small door at the top of the cage. I lunged, getting my face and front paws out quickly—I couldn't wait to be free of this horrible trap! But just as fast I felt his meaty palm press the top of my head back down into the cage. He shoved the fish head in, then slammed the small door and fastened it tight.

"That should keep," he said, wiping his hands on his

pants as he stood. "Look sharp, won't you? Me mates will be round to have a gander later."

He moved away from the cage and back down the row of stalls, toward the open doorway. I could now see light pouring in from outside as the sun came up and the docks came alive. Around me the animals started to wake and make their usual noises. I glanced down the rows of stalls and realized that I was now like them: trapped and kept here against my will. What did the sailor mean that his mates would be by to have a look at me? What was he keeping me here for?

I turned round and round, searching for a way to escape. But bars met me at every side. I pushed against them with the top of my head and scratched at them, hissing. With one paw I reached out again, grasping at straws of hay. It was useless!

I paced inside the tiny cage, turning circles around the fish head that had been left for me. While I had woken hungry, I now had no appetite. I had to get out! I was due back on the docks to await my own crew, or for Colin to find me and bring me to them. No one would know where I was, tucked away in a cage in the back of this livestock barn. I began to cry again, meowing at the top of my lungs, but this time I was sure no one could hear my mews over the snuffs and sounds of the other animals. I was trapped, and there seemed no way out.

CHAPTER 30

LANDLOCKED

How many hours passed as I sat, paced, meowed, and generally fretted inside that small cage, I do not know. I only had the sun as my guide, and I watched as it moved from the doorway of the livestock barn to directly overhead to around behind. At one point, about midmorning, a man did come through and throw some feed to the animals in the stalls, but they were in the front portion of the barn, not tucked into the back as I was. I meowed as strongly as I could, but his head never even turned in my direction before he was out again, sliding the great door shut behind him.

The fish head the old sailor had given me was starting to let off a stinking smell. I tried to take a few bites, but in my general sadness I had no stomach for it and decided instead to bury it under the hay beneath my feet. As the barn grew dim and then dark, I waited, pacing in my tiny prison, for the old sailor to return, but he seemed to have forgotten me. How terrible! Worse than being caged was being locked up and forgotten. Would I starve to death here—never to see my mates again?

At long last I put my head down on my paws and fell into a restless sleep, thinking over my current quandary and my adventures at sea. At every turn, no matter how perilous, there had always been a way to survive. But now, in this trap, I could see no way out. I wondered what the captain would do, how he would solve this, but came up with no answers.

I woke to a shrill sound that set me instantly on my four paws. A whistle! Could it be the captain, calling me? I paced the cage and reached my paws through the bars again, grasping at the hay with my claws. Had I dreamed the sound of the whistle, or was it real? The barn had grown dark and the animals now seemed to be sleeping, so I perked my ears high and listened. It came again, clearly, as if the man himself was walking just outside—the high-pitched fast whistle. Oh, Captain! He was searching for me, but how would he ever find me here?

I set to meowing and growling as loudly as I could, aiming my voice to the doors, where the whistle had come from. All he needed to do was hear me and I knew I would be rescued! But as the minutes ticked away, and my voice grew hoarse and raspy, there was no sign of him at the door. I still continued to mew feebly, pausing to see if I could hear his whistle in return, but it did not come.

Then, just as I was about to give up hope, I saw the big door to the livestock barn slide open and some figures appear in shadow. I was saved! I knew the captain would come for me, and at last he had.

But as the figures drew near, I saw all at once that my rescue was not to be. I looked up eagerly, expecting to see the captain's warm face and blue eyes, but was greeted instead with the gnarled face of the old sailor who had trapped me.

"There he be, mates," he said, lifting the cage from the barn floor and holding it up. "A healthy one, just a lad still—lots of years left in 'im."

One of the strangers with him held up a lantern and peered into my cage. "He looks fit. How much you want? Say he's a mouser, that so?"

"He's caught all type of vermin—you know the boss won't have any eating through his feed. This one's a ratter, I swear on it," said the old sailor. The cheek of him, I thought, when I realized what he was doing! I was a ratter, to be sure, but this old sailor had never seen me catch anything.

"Funny smell off 'im, innit?" the man behind the sailor said. "Smells o' rot, he does."

"Ah, that's just his dinner—fish he loves, just that, mates, nothing more," the old salt was quick to explain.

"Has he white paws on?" The first man leaned in again with the lantern. "Ha! And you say he's a ratter; there's no chance of that!"

"Come on, Henry, let's off—this old salt's having a laugh," the other man said, pulling the fellow with the lantern away from my cage.

"I tell you, as I live, he's a ratter, he is!" the old sailor exclaimed, watching the two men as they walked toward the doors. "But the price, don't you want to know the price of 'im?"

But the men just tossed a laugh over their shoulders, and I watched as the door slid open and they left without a backward glance.

"You stupid animal," the old sailor hissed at me through the bars. I backed away from him, to the other side of the cage. "Laughing at me now, are they? I'll get a pretty penny for you, I will." With that he dropped my cage with a thump back down onto the hay and walked away without a glance, through the doors and no doubt in search of another buyer.

When the cage was dropped, I thought I heard the top door rattle a bit on its hinges, and I reached up with my paw now to feel around the edges. It was securely closed, and I could not reason how the man had opened it before. I lay back down, my head on my paws, and found my mind traveling to the day aboard the *Bristol* when Leo Bear had shown me the snakes in their cage. I had never figured how he had managed to get that snake up to the deck without setting them all loose, but now I puzzled it over.

Suddenly I stood up straight. He must have opened the cage, and then closed it again. It was the only way! And if he could do it, with his big, clumsy paws . . . I gingerly felt around the top of the cage again, to where the hinges were, then moved my paws over to the other side.

There—a small metal pole was pushed through a hole. If I could move it back, the whole door would be free to swing open. I began to work it with my paws but found that my claws could get no hold on the metal. After batting at it for some time, I felt it move, perhaps only slightly.

I took a break and paced around the bars when my shoulders and legs grew weary. The sailors had been right; there was a foul smell coming from the bottom of my cage. I put my paws up again and continued to work on the small metal pole, moving it only slightly when my claws caught it just so. Leo Bear must have worked long and hard to get that snake out—I was only realizing now how much he must have disliked me to persevere!

But I vowed not to spend another night in this trap, and worked the metal latch until I felt my claws might bleed.

CHAPTER 31

ONE FOR ALL, AND ALL FOR ONE

When the livestock barn door slid open again, letting in the morning light, I watched with fear, thinking that the old sailor would be back with more buyers who might take me aboard their ship. But instead it was just the man who fed the other animals. I was too weak and hungry to meow for him, my throat too dry to make any sound over a raspy mew. I lay in the bottom of the cage waiting for him to go before I set back to my work on the metal pole.

I put my face to the bars and tried to bite the pole, but I could get no traction, so instead I kept to my claws, batting it just fractions at a time. It was moving, and I could see that I was almost there, almost to freedom. If only I could move the metal before the old sailor returned . . .

As the sun rose higher in the sky, now over the barn, I worked and worked, taking no breaks. In my imagination I again heard the captain's trademark whistle for me—short and fast, calling me to his side. Oh, what I wouldn't give to hear that sound just one more time! I sighed and put my claws up to the metal pole, grasping over and over. The sound came again and I stood stock-still. Was it my imagination this time, or a real sound? Had I gone mad, like poor Sean had done on the longboat? I perked my ears and paced, listening, but heard only the bustle of the docks coming in through the open door, now in full force—horse hooves and men hollering, all manner of business going on. But no whistle.

Just when I was determined to declare myself done for, the whistle came once more—there was no mistaking it! I found the strength I needed. My paws flew up, furiously batting at the metal with a speed I did not know that I possessed. Then, with a squeak of metal on metal, the bar at last slid free, and I pushed my nose against the door, flipping it open fast with a metal clang. I leapt from the cage like a flying fish off the surface of the sea and lit through the barn as if Leo Bear himself were chasing me! Out the doors and onto the cobblestone street, racing to the docks without any mind to the horses and carts that passed over me as I slid in the still-muddy roads.

Up and down the Coburn Dock I went, chasing the sound of that whistle, but I did not see the captain or Colin or my mates. Instead, horses and carts clomped by me; men loading and unloading the ships yelled to each other. I stopped in the noise and confusion to perk my ears and listen only for one sound, blocking everything else out. At last it came again! But I had moved farther from it than I had been when I was in the barn.

I raced back to the top of Coburn Dock, where it met the streets, and searched the crowds for any sign of the captain, dodging and weaving through the footfalls of the sailors as they came to and fro. I studied each boot that passed me, hoping to recognize one as that of Colin or the captain himself. But soon the boots began to blur and all looked alike; I wouldn't have known the captain's feet if he'd stepped over me. Now I was frantic—if I missed my chance to answer his whistle, would he ever come again? Or would I be left here forever, on my own on the docks?

My eyes seemed to betray me when, at last, I spotted a most beautiful sight: Melissa! Could it be? In a light blue dress and bonnet to match, a hand held at her forehead to block the sun as she searched the docks. What was she looking for? The *Melissa Rae,* perhaps—or any sign of her father? My heart ached to think that she did not know—how could she know?—that her father's ship was lost, and that he had been taken away to who knows where.

I worked my way through the crowd, weaving between feet and staying close to the curb to avoid the horses' hooves. I kept my eyes glued on Melissa, believing it was she who had whistled, until I drew closer and saw a man move out from behind her, a tall man with a hat upon his head, a small braid of light hair, a flash of ice-blue eyes. The captain! Wearing the same as he had worn the day I'd seen him last, and looking none the better, but there, all the same! He raised his fingers to his mouth and let out the whistle I longed to hear, now so close to me that I could nearly feel it.

I kept my eyes upon them as I raced, without caution, through the legs and boots that came at me, to Melissa's side, and it was she who saw me first. "Father! It's Jacob, it is him! He is so changed, I barely know him!" She scooped me up, my muddy paws and all, and held me to her.

"It is indeed," the captain said, his eyes getting that crinkled look they only took on when he was very, very happy. He put a hand under my chin and looked into my face. "How you've survived days and nights on these rough docks, there's no way to know, but well done, lad, well done."

With Melissa's arms tight around me, my heart beat fast and my purring rattled in my chest. I could not remember a time when I had been happier. Only moments before, I had been trapped in a cage, and now I was back in the arms of the girl who had saved me as a runt, and with her father, my captain. How quickly my fortune had changed!

The captain guided us across the busy street and into the city of Liverpool, walking with his head lowered and at a fast pace. His limp was noticeable now, as he moved quickly, and it brought back many bad memories. But those were banished when I looked into his ruddy face and saw the smile that was plastered there. I looked up to Melissa's face and took in her pink cheeks and glossy hair—whatever had ailed her when we set sail seemed to have passed, and she was well. I nestled my head into the space beneath her chin and purred my delight.

As we rounded a corner and onto another busy street, a small boy—smaller than Melissa—was waving something over his head and yelling loud enough to startle me. "Heroes at sea! Read all about the mystery island!"

The captain stopped, dead in his tracks, to look at what the boy was holding. He took a paper from the stack next to the boy and held it up, showing Melissa. And there, on the very front, was a fine sketch that captured the likeness of the captain himself! The captain dropped a coin into the boy's cup.

"Heroes at sea! Oh, Father!" Melissa leaned in and hugged him, sandwiching me between them.

When last I had seen my captain, he was being led away in shackles. Now a hero? Soon I would know the whole story of what had happened to my mates while we were parted.

"Come now, we mustn't be later than we already are." The captain tucked the paper beneath one arm and held Melissa's elbow with the other as we moved through the crowds. I looked back over Melissa's shoulder and saw many other passersby picking up the same paper from the young boy.

Within a few more turns we had arrived at a set of stone stairs that led up to a fine home, with planters full of flowers in the front windows and a flag flying outside the red door. As we entered, I was struck with a blast of warm air and divine smells—cooked meats and breads. My mouth began to water so, I thought I might drool. Melissa quickly bustled down a long, wood-paneled hallway that opened into a grand room brimming with people, with a warm fire in the corner and a feast laid out upon the table. It was as close to heaven as any sea cat could wish for on land. There was only one thing missing. . . .

All in the room turned to greet us as we entered, and a cheer quickly went up when they saw that I was in Melissa's arms—"Ho, ho, hooray!"—and cups were raised. I dug my claws into Melissa's shoulder, a bit overwhelmed at the greeting and searching the faces before me. Then happiness washed over me as my eyes found them, my best mates, Chippy and Moses, standing at the long table. Their clothing was fresh, their faces clear and happy. As if by some miracle, they had escaped the terrible men who had led them away from the *Bristol*. And not only that, they looked perhaps better than I had seen them since we set sail!

Moses moved around the table and came to Melissa, taking me from her arms. I noted, with embarrassment, that my paws had left dirt on the front of her very pretty blue dress, but she seemed not to mind one bit.

"If a cat has nine lives, this one must be on his last, I do declare!" Moses grinned, squeezing me a bit too tightly. "I've never been so pleased to see an old sea hand such as you."

Just then the captain pulled the paper from under his

arm and slapped it down onto the table. "There it is in black and white, men."

Chippy was the first to pick up the newspaper. "A handsome likeness," he said, before going on to read the article aloud for everyone to hear.

I did not understand every aspect of the case, but from what I could gather, my mates had been led straight to jail off the *Bristol* until a judge could hear the charges against them. While I had been locked in a cage in the livestock barn, Chippy, Moses, and the captain had spent the night in their own cage: jail. I felt quite terrible for them all at once.

But when they had appeared before the judge the following morning and the case had been heard, the facts held up in a way that was quite unexpected. Because the captain had been unconscious when he was loaded into the longboat, the judge declared that he was not accountable for his actions. He had not deserted his ship. Nor could the mutiny charge be proven, as no crew member from the *Melissa Rae* had returned to give evidence. The judge dismissed the charges against the men and ordered that the remaining crew be paid for their work by the Archer Shipping Company.

The article went on to describe in great detail our adventures at sea and aboard the *Bristol*. In fact, the majority of words were given over to our account of being on the island, and how we survived there.

As Chippy read aloud, I watched the captain from

where I sat, curled on Moses's lap. He was obviously pleased about the outcome, but when Chippy reached the part about the *Melissa Rae* being lost at sea, I saw a cloudy look pass over the captain's face. Melissa came to stand beside him and put her hand upon his shoulder, where he reached up to hold it. I realized that even if the law did not find him guilty, he held himself responsible for the lives of his crew, even terrible Archer.

As the men discussed the case, and the outcome, I looked about the room to the other people who were collected there in our honor. Chippy's wife, I was much surprised to learn, was a dainty lass, fair and fine of face and figure. She was delicate and small where he was large and rough, but their affection for each other was evident. Moses's lady was actually smaller than the man himself, if that can be believed, not much larger than Melissa. She called to me and, with a bit of roast beef from her plate and a scratch under my chin, won my heart instantly.

As food and drink were passed about, the newspaper article was read aloud again and again. I curled into a spot under the table, my belly now filled to bursting, listening to the words roll over me, of our story and our adventures. Of course, it seemed a great oversight to have not included even one mention of me, the ship's cat, and my role in all this, but I suppose one cannot expect every good deed to go noticed. Though a small drawing of myself in the newspaper might have been a welcome addition.

As the group talked and celebrated, I did note that Chippy's hands were busy with something, a bit of brown leather, perhaps something for Melissa, who flitted in and out of the room, an apron tied over her blue dress, waiting on everyone and performing as quite the lady of the house. My lids grew heavy in the warmth of the crowded room, and I drifted into a light nap, imagining us back aboard the *Melissa Rae*, myself curled under the stove in the galley.

When I woke, the room had somewhat cleared, with only Moses, Chippy, and their wives, along with the captain, still there. I assumed Melissa was tuckered out from the excitement of the day. Lanterns and candles were lit all around. I heard Chippy's gruff voice call out, "Tibbs! Now, where has that cat got himself?"

I appeared from under the table by his side, and he was startled to see me so fast. "Must think I've a bite for him!" Chippy laughed, patting his lap. I knew this meant to jump up, and so I did, purring and receiving a lovely scratch behind the ears. "If ever we are parted from our ship's cat again, this will bring you home, mate," Chippy explained. He held up the braided leather band he had been working on, and I noted that now a dangling tag carved of wood hung from it. He secured it round my neck.

"What's it there?" Mrs. MacNeil asked, looking at the tag.

"'Prop. Captain N. Natick,'" Moses read out. "Means he's the property of Captain Natick—as if any man can own a sea cat." He put his hand on top of my head and smoothed over my back, all the way to the end of my tail.

"I never thought I would see the equal to our Mrs. Tibbs, God rest her, but I was wrong, and I freely say it." Moses looked a bit choked up, and his wife placed a hand on his arm, perhaps pulling him from his bad memories, reminding him that we were now safe on land. "To her son, Jacob Tibbs. Long may he walk the decks. Hear, hear!" He raised a cup, and our mates also did, cheering for me three times. To hear myself mentioned in the same breath as my mother made me swell with pride. I must admit, the chocolate color of the leather was a fetching complement to my yellow fur, and I did change my opinion of collars on that day.

"He's well off with that, as we'll be down to the docks tomorrow, men, Mr. Tibbs along," Captain Natick said.

I felt my blood run cold at the thought of returning to the docks. After all that had happened, why would the captain want to go there?

"With this along, you shan't have trouble finding a vessel, I think, Captain," Moses said, lifting the paper and pointing to the pencil drawing of the man himself.

"Aye, but I'll only sign on to a ship that will take my full crew—first mate Charles MacNeil"—the captain paused and raised his glass—"cook Mr. Moses"—he raised his glass again before going on—"and the finest ship's cat in Liverpool, perhaps the entire Atlantic: Mr. Jacob Tibbs."

I sat up at the sound of my name then, feeling the weight of my new collar around my neck. So the captain meant to go to sea again! I studied his face as he talked and celebrated. He was a true man of the waves, and I

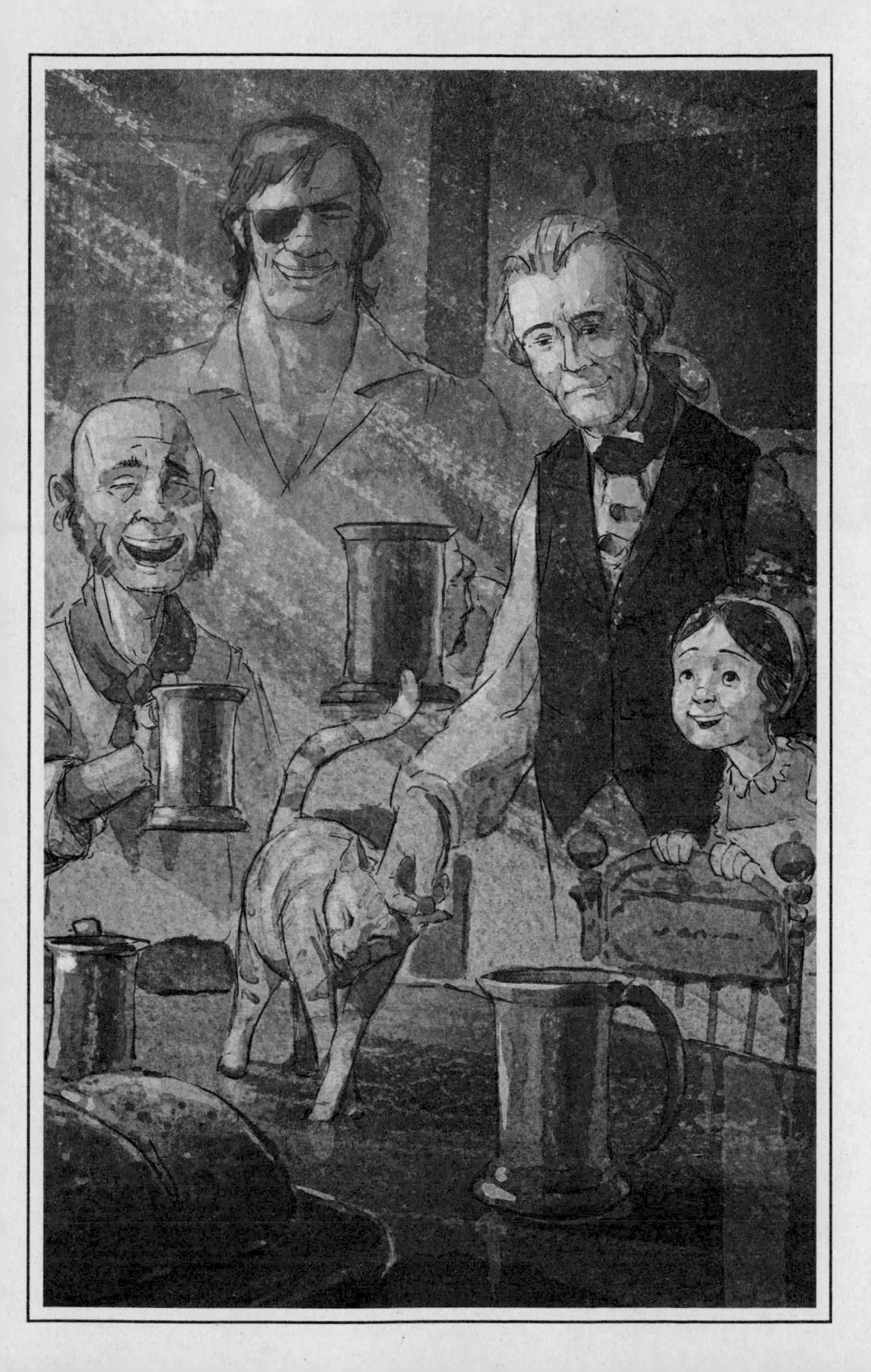

trusted him to crew up a ship with sailors who knew their way. He would never allow a tragedy like that we had seen on the *Melissa Rae*. Never again. He would sail, as he should, on a new ship, and he meant to take us with him.

Though the memories of the *Melissa Rae* and all that befell us that trip out remained fresh in my mind, I could hardly wait to have my paws back on deck, breathing in the sea air and standing at my captain's side. Working a new ship, patrolling the hold, napping in the galley, checking the weather at the bow each morning. She would be a fine ship, perhaps more so even than the *Melissa Rae*, perhaps as big as the *Bristol*. Who knew what great adventures awaited a crew such as ours?

I moved from Chippy's lap up onto the wooden table, where I sat, quite proudly and sphinxlike, directly in the middle, to the laughter of my mates. But no one asked me off, so there I stayed, among them, while they admired, to a one, my new collar, reading it aloud as the celebration wore into the night.

Prop. Captain N. Natick. Never was I so proud in my life.

AUTHOR'S NOTE

In the mid-1800s, when packet ships were used to move goods across the Atlantic, most vessels had a cat on board. The cat was meant to keep the vermin population under control and was not considered a pet. But sailors, being superstitious, began to think that some cats were more than just mousers. The sailors believed that certain cat breeds were "lucky," that their presence promised a safe journey, or their markings could foretell what kind of mousers they would become. Some sailors even believed that cats could predict the weather and send secret messages to the sailors to warn them of rough seas—like when a ship's cat paced the boards instead of climbing the ratlines, they were sure to have high winds. The best captain's cats were bred for their skill and purchased by other vessels.

While Jacob Tibbs is a fictional cat, there are many real cats who served on ships and gained widespread fame for their bravery and seafaring exploits. Blackie, a British cat aboard HMS *Prince of Wales*, was photographed with Prime Minister Winston Churchill in 1941. Convoy, who traveled on HMS *Hermione*, was thought to be such a superior captain's cat, he was given his own sailor's kit—

complete with a tiny hammock in the sailors' quarters! Jenny, a brave ship's cat aboard the *Titanic*, gave birth to a litter of kittens just before that vessel met an iceberg on a cold, dark night in 1912. But perhaps most famous is Mrs. Chippy, who, in 1914, sailed aboard Shackleton's *Endurance* to the Antarctic until the ship became icebound. Blackie, Convoy, Jenny, Mrs. Chippy, and other real-hero cats-o'-sea served as the inspiration for Mr. Jacob Tibbs and his adventure with his fellow sailors.

In researching this book, I came across countless fantastic captain's cats. I also learned a great deal about life aboard a ship in the 1800s and sailors' many superstitions. Here are a few of the questions I'm frequently asked about Jacob and his mates, and what life might have been like on the *Melissa Rae*:

☸ How long was a typical journey?

In the mid-1800s, the only way to cross the Atlantic was in a sailing ship, either built for cargo, like the packet ship *Melissa Rae*, or a passenger ship. Depending on the weather, currents, and winds, crossing from Liverpool, England, to New York could take anywhere from several weeks to two months, with ships covering between 100–150 miles a day. The return trip was usually faster, taking advantage of the westerlies (winds that blow from the west), and could be made in as little as twenty days.

☸ What were the different roles on the ship?

Everyone on board a packet ship worked incredibly hard, starting with the captain. The captain is charged with overseeing the safety of everyone on board, as well as the daily running of the ship. Below the captain come the sailors, ranked in this order:

First Mate: Second in command, the first mate assists the captain in making all decisions from navigation to work shifts. If the captain is incapacitated, the first mate assumes the responsibilities of captain.

Second Mate: Assistant to the first mate, the second mate is usually in charge of record keeping and is assigned the first mate's duties when the first mate is unavailable.

Able-Bodied Sailors, or ABS/general class: These are the working men of the ship, including cabin boys as young as twelve years old. Within this class, there is a division of duty, with some sailors being better at rigging and others at deck work.

Ship's Cook: The ship's cook is in charge of cooking, serving, cleaning and sometimes acting as the ship's doctor if one is not available. This position was often filled by an older sailor who was no longer fit, for whatever reason, to serve above deck.

Carpenter: A sailor trained in woodworking who could make any repairs on board. A ship's carpenter was commonly nicknamed Chippy because of wood chips he left behind.

☸ What was life like aboard a real packet ship?

Perhaps Ralph Waldo Emerson answered this question best when he wrote this aboard the *New York* in 1833:

"The road from Liverpool to New York, as they who have traveled it well know, is very long, crooked, rough, and eminently disagreeable."

Life aboard a packet ship in the mid-1800s was not for the timid! The ships were cramped, with the majority of the space taken up with cargo, along with the supplies needed for the journey. The sailors' quarters were dark, damp, and infested with pests—from the rats that Jacob Tibbs hunts to roaches, fleas, and lice. Sailors were frequently ill and alternated between being anxious about the weather to suffering extreme boredom. The work was hard, sleep was scarce, and there was little healthy food. You can see why having a lucky cat like Jacob on board was a welcome distraction.

☸ Were there other animals aboard, or just cats?

Though almost every ship had a cat or two, some carried other animals. Dogs were sometimes brought aboard—but mostly as companions since they were not very useful at catching rats or predicting the weather, as cats were believed to be. Livestock such as cows, goats, and pigs were also occasionally brought aboard to serve as a food source. Keeping livestock on a packet ship was complicated since it required having a place for the animals to stay and enough food to feed them during the journey. With no other way to store meat (unless it was dried), bringing animals aboard was a smart way to provide fresh food.

☸ What was a storm like on board a packet ship?

The hold on a packet ship was usually filled with cargo—mail and other items being shipped between countries. If the hold was full of something heavy—like iron, gunpowder, or bars of metal—then the ship would be a bit slower on the journey. But it might also be safer, as a bottom-heavy ship was harder to capsize. Passenger vessels, with no cargo to weigh them down, often had a rougher journey during storms.

☸ How often did a castaway situation happen? And how would they be rescued?

Maritime history is full of stories about castaways, each account more harrowing than the last. If castaways were lucky enough to find land, they then needed to locate food and fresh water. But their survival was still uncertain, and many castaways succumbed to their injuries, starvation, and dehydration. Being rescued was another dilemma. Without the benefit of search planes or helicopters, the castaways would need to wait for a passing ship, which were few and far between, especially if the desert island was nowhere near a trade route.

☸ What was it like on the docks of Liverpool and New York City in the 1800s?

Both in England and the United States, the docks were a furiously busy place. Packets and passenger vessels were constantly docking, unloading, reloading, and heading back out to sea. Just like an airport, the docks were crowded with people and baggage. You could also find horses and carriages, stray animals, and sailors of all ages and nationalities. Nearby were inns and shops that would provide the sailors and ships with everything they needed for their journeys. These businesses contributed to building the towns around them into the modern-day cities we now know.

ACKNOWLEDGMENTS

A deep bow of gratitude to my early readers:

Holly Black
Pamela Bunn
Cecil Castellucci
Nanci Katz Ellis
Barry Goldblatt
Jo Knowles
Melanie Cecka Nolan
Ginee Seo
Joan Slattery
Erin Zimring

Thank you to my family—Damon, August, Polly, Betty, and Jean—for reading many versions of this novel over the past fifteen years. To Mrs. Perez and her class, thank you for the lovely drawings of Jacob & Co.

And many thanks to my agent, Brenda Bowen, who may not be the biggest fan of cats but proved to be a very big supporter of Jacob Tibbs.

In loving memory of Arthur Bear, Wrassman, Pyewackett, and Jake Ross, for whom Jacob is named.